THE BRIDEZILLA WHO STOLE CHRISTMAS

A Teddy and Pip Story

By Lisa Maddock

First published by Dog Ear Publishing
4010 W. 86th Street, Ste H
Indianapolis, IN 46268
www.dogearpublishing.net

ISBN: 978-160844-2584

This book is printed on acid-free paper.
This book is a work of fiction. Places, events, and situations in this book are purely
fictional and any resemblance to actual persons, living or dead, is coincidental.

Printed in the United States of America

To Allison and Bill

Table of Contents

PROLOGUE

In the quiet town of Westerfield, on a gray December afternoon, a certain guinea pig, having grown tired of the daytime soaps and game shows, expertly pushed the channel-changing button with his little paw. Colors and pictures flipped by. Faster and faster he flipped through many channels, watching the humans go by, doing silly human things. Quite by accident, his paw slipped and the screen settled onto something he had not seen before today. (This was unusual because Pip watched a lot of television.)

Teddy joined his friend in front of the screen. The two of them stared, stared for quite a while in silence as the show went on. The program was new, but what it was all about was familiar.

When it was over, Pip made a smallish gasp and looked at Teddy. A tiny light bulb had lit in his guinea pig mind. He understood now. He understood something that he did not at all wish to. It made sense. Surely it explained what had been going on.

He looked at Teddy, shaking his head slowly back and forth. Teddy slumped, his furry head resting on his paws. Teddy had come to the same scary realization. Both sighed, soft guinea pig sighs, and Pip turned off the television with a final half-hearted push of his paw. No more TV today, he thought. He had seen enough.

What in the world were they going to do?

Best friend Amelia... *had turned into a Bride Monster.*

CAST OF CHARACTERS

Readers, this is Molly. If you did not catch my first story, you will not know who everyone is, so here is a helpful list. If you did read my first story, you can skip over this page, because you might be thinking, "Well, duh, I already know all of that," and I don't want to make anyone upset or confused. Actually, there *are* some new people in this story, so maybe you should just read it either way.

Molly Jane Fisher
That's me. I am an almost-ten-year-old detective girl who loves animals. I especially love guinea pigs. I have a parakeet named Tweets who likes to land on people's heads. I have thirteen Grandmas; three are related, and ten are actually adopted. Most of them live at Shady Acres.

Amelia Dearling
Amelia is a famous novel writer who lives in my family's garage apartment. Amelia is engaged to Wally. She is a very nice person who loves guinea pigs. Amelia has two guinea pigs, Teddy and Pip.

Wally (Professor Walter Holmby)
Wally teaches Economics at Princeton University. He is very smart and kind. He has a bushy mustache and a warm

chuckle. He always knows the right thing to say. He loves Amelia very much. He also loves Teddy and Pip very much.

Teddy (Theodore Hamilton III)
Teddy is the 'boss of the guinea pigs' because he lived with Wally before Pip did. Teddy has an all-black face and white and tan on the rest of him. He is usually reasonable and always sweet.

Pip (Pippen)
Pip is the feisty little guinea pig of the pair. Pip is mostly white, but has black and brown patches around his eyes. Pip screams a lot, but his screaming is not really loud. He can be really loud if he does guinea pig noises, though, so look out! Pip writes songs. (Oh, did I mention that Teddy and Pip can talk? They can. That's pretty important, amazing, and cool.)

Mom Jane (Jane Fisher)
This is my mom. She is the greatest. She is called 'Mom Jane' by Teddy and Pip. They do not get along with her. There is no really good reason. She put them in a bucket when she was cleaning for them one time and they can't get over it.

Daddy (Dan Fisher)
My dad is allergic to furry animals, so I do not have any furry pets, just Tweets (my parakeet, who I love). Daddy is a computer guy, and also he does wood-working stuff. He is a great dad. The guinea pigs think he is a very cool guy.

Evelyn
She is Amelia's sister, who is helping her plan the wedding. We are all afraid of her, I think.

Sunny
This is the wedding planner. I have not met her, but the guinea pigs do not approve of her.

The Best Friends Club
At the start of this story, the Best Friends Club includes Teddy and Pip, me, Wally and Amelia.

A Christmas Poem
By Molly J. Fisher

Days before Christmas, and all through my house,
I was doing some homework, Mom was ironing a blouse.
The lights were a' twinkling on our Christmas tree
And Daddy out shopping, mysteriously...

When what to my wondering ears should I hear,
But a telephone call from a neighbor so dear.
Amelia was desperate for help it did seem
With guinea pigs showing no holiday gleam.

"Could Molly come quickly, and quiet them, please?"
I said I would do so—it would be a breeze.
My neighbor, you see, has two guinea pigs rare,
Cute as buttons they are, but, believe if you dare,

These guinea pigs talk just like humans can do!
Sometimes what they say will give some pause to you...
There was a big mystery, not so long ago,
Involving Amelia and Wally, her beau.

We sleuthed out some lies and outright thievery,
Then the two of them knew that a wedding must be.
But something was just not quite right with them all
So 'Molly to the rescue', an order never too tall.

For best friends we all are and have been since that day,
And with any luck, best friends we will stay.
So I headed out bravely through fresh fallen snow
And knocked on the door and said, "Well, hello!"

What's next, you will have to read all about...
So to all a good read—this is Molly—over and out.

CHAPTER 1 –

Molly in the Interrogation Chair

December 22, late afternoon
*COUNTDOWN TO CHRISTMAS: 25 24 23 **22** 21 20 19 18 17*

Mom handed Amelia a cup of tea in a Christmas mug as I edged into the living room unnoticed. I sat on the floor next to the sofa, not saying a word, and waited. Christmas music played softly in the background, the tree had lit lights and there were presents under it. It was gently snowing outside, which is not always the case where we live. Except for the fact that Amelia had just finished crying (or maybe she wasn't quite finished yet, she was still looking very upset) it would have been a perfect day-before-Christmas-Eve scene at my house.

Amelia Dearling is a famous novel writer, and our garage-apartment renter. If that sounds like a strange combination to you, you're right. There is a really good reason for Amelia to live here and that is called privacy. She came to New Jersey to get away from snoopy fans and people like that so she could write her books in peace. After a year and a half of being our renter, and after we shared a great big mystery and adventure together last summer, she isn't just our renter anymore, Amelia Dearling is our friend.

Amelia and her fiancé, Wally, are getting married soon. I am super happy for them. In fact, I am a big part of the reason that they are getting married at all. If you want to know the details, please read my first story (It's really good!). Just for the record, I definitely, totally, would not do anything to mess up the wedding or stop them from getting married. For some reason, I feel like I need to say that.

Wally and Amelia share two amazing guinea pigs who can talk. Really, it's true. Teddy and Pip can talk. They have their very own room in the little garage apartment, including an amazing two-story house with ramps to climb up and down. Teddy and Pip weren't in the room with Amelia and Mom, but I had to mention them to you. When you know talking guinea pigs, you can hardly keep them out of a conversation. And since I am only allowed to talk about them with a few people, and you readers, I take every opportunity I can get. I am sure we will *all* be talking about them very soon.

"Wally is on his way," Mom was saying in that soothy way she talks when she is around anyone who is upset. "I am sure that we will sort all of this out, Amelia, and it will be *all right*."

Amelia sniffled and nodded her head, jiggling her teacup and spilling a glob of tea on the chair. "Oh, Jane, I am so sorry," she mumbled. "So clumsy of me…" she stood up, looking uncertain about what to do next.

Mom gestured to Amelia to sit down on the sofa while she set a coaster on the coffee table nearby. She smiled and told her not to worry about the chair. Amelia was lucky. If *I* had spilled something on that fancy schmancy chair it would've pretty much been the end of the world.

I gave up my hidey spot and went to the kitchen to get a wet washcloth for Mom to deal with the spill, because it is always good to get extra points at Christmastime, right? And I was apparently in some kind of double-secret trouble.

"Oh, Molly, thank you." Mom took the cloth from me, looking relieved about being able to scrub at her chair and also because I was there now to take over with Amelia. "Look, Amelia, Molly's here."

Amelia looked at me and tried to smile, but she did not quite make it there. "Molly. Oh Molly dear. Thank you for coming down. I did not mean for you to be... to be interrupted in your... I surely don't want you to think that this is... is some kind of a... or that we are *ganging up*... on *you*... or *anything*. I just need to know what happened." Amelia bit her lip and her hand headed for the teacup again.

Mom, brushing at the upholstery with the washcloth, watched out of the corner of her eye.

Ganging up on me? About what?

Ten minutes ago, I was upstairs in my room, putting the finishing touches on some Christmas cards for all of my adopted Grandmas at Shady Acres. Each was different and extra- special— for each different and extra-special Grandma. There was kind of a lot of glitter spilled on my bed and all over the floor. My parakeet, Tweets, who had been flying around and landing on my head as I worked, had left a little trail of presents of his own around the room that I needed to clean up. I was just about to start on that not-fun project when Mom knocked on the door, stepped in and closed it behind her.

"Molly, Amelia is downstairs in a terrible state. She needs to talk to you. Honey, what happened?" Mom's eyes darted quickly all around the room, then settled on me. I guess she decided that the problem with Amelia was more important than birdie poop or a glitter mess. Which meant that the Amelia problem was a really big one.

I stared at her with my blankest look. The blankness was real. I had no idea in the whole wide world what she was talking about. Blankety blank Molly. Then my mind, which cannot stay blank for long, shifted to the guinea pigs and I got totally panicky and really scared. "Are Teddy and Pip okay?"

Mom gave a sigh and shook her head. "This has nothing to do with those animals," she said a bit impatiently. "This is about Amelia's wedding."

The panic went away and blankness returned. "Amelia's wedding," I said with a shrug. "I don't know anything much about Amelia's wedding; except that I got to see her dress one day and I told her it was pretty. That's all I know. Is something wrong with her dress?"

"Molly, seriously…"

"Mom, I *am* being totally serious. What would I know about the wedding?"

Mom looked like she was trying to decide if I was holding out on her. "Come down to the living room and talk to Amelia. She has asked to see you, so… there must be something. Please take care of that bird mess first, though, will you?"

So, there I was, with Amelia's teary eyes on me but with no idea what her upsetness had to *do* with me. I felt really bad for her. I like Amelia a whole lot. I waited for her to tell me what it was that she thought I did, didn't do, said, didn't say, or whatever about her wedding, so I could tell her I was sorry, or that I didn't mean it, or whatever and we could get past this.

When neither of us made a single peep for about a minute (and that minute seemed like a whole year), Amelia said, "Wally received a phone call this morning—from my sister, Evelyn. Evelyn is very upset after a conversation that she had… with you."

Mom and Amelia were both looking at me now. I started to feel sweaty even though I didn't know why I should be.

"She has cancelled all of the wedding plans," Amelia continued, her voice getting tight. "It appears that my wedding... is cancelled." She tried to laugh but it sounded kind of crazy.

I looked hard at Amelia after that. My jaw dropped way open, too.

"*She* cancelled *your* wedding?" I asked, my voice whispery and shocked. "But she can't do that! Can she do that?" I looked at my mom, who raised her eyebrows, then back at Amelia.

Amelia did a laugh-snort-cry, and then reached for a Kleenex. "Apparently, she can. She called the wedding planner and told her to call it all off," Amelia said. "The wedding planner *is* a personal friend of my sister's..." Her voice trailed off and she reached for her tea.

"But, still..." I said, shaking my head. "I don't understand why she would think that she could... or why she *would*..." My voice trailed off too.

"She said that after talking to *you* she understood that it was what *I* wanted," Amelia said quietly. After that she just kept looking at me and looking at me. It was not a comfortable time.

None of us said anything for another long time. Mom and Amelia both kept looking at me, waiting for me to crack. I wished I could disappear. My mind was kind of spinning around trying to remember that icky conversation with her scary sister.

"Please, Molly, if you could tell us what you and Evelyn said to each other, maybe we can figure this out together. I would certainly ask her myself, but she has left for London with her husband and is not answering her cell phone."

I realized then that Amelia did not sound mad, not really, her voice was more pleading, and that made me feel worse.

"I'll try," I said, shifting uncomfortably in my seat. "I don't really remember everything we said. It didn't make much sense to me at the time, the things she was saying."

"All you can do is try, Molly," Mom said. "Tell us what you *do* remember."

(Readers, fasten your seatbelts! We are going to do some backwards time-traveling so we can relive a memory of mine. It might help to close your eyes real tight. It will only take a few seconds. Are you ready? Let's go!)

CHAPTER 2 –

Angry Evelyn

We Travel Back to December 20, late morning
*COUNTDOWN TO CHRISTMAS: 25 24 23 22 21 **20** 19 18 17*

I had been having a really good morning. I was watching the guinea pigs for Amelia while she ran a quick errand in town. After putting on their jingling Christmas hats, I was sitting on the wheely chair in Teddy and Pip's room, being the audience. Pip was singing a Christmas song he had made up just for me:

Christmas is good when best friends are near.
I am happy Molly Jane is here.
Christmas is best when hats have bells.
Joy to the whole world, my heart swells!

Dad brings Christmas to Pip and Ted-dy.
Tree and lights and music and glee.
Christmas is best when hats have bells.
Joy to the world... Pip's whole heart swells!

Teddy accompanied the song by tilting his head this way and that so the bells on his hat jingled to the beat. It was pretty darned adorable. It was the best song I think he ever made up, and I clapped and cheered.

The door in the other room opened without a knock. I figured it was just Amelia so I stayed where I was. I couldn't wait to tell her about Pip's song.

It wasn't Amelia.

"Amelia?!" The sharp voice made guinea pigs run for cover, hats jingling wildly as they disappeared into plastic igloos.

"EVELYN! NO GOOD SISTER! SAVE US MOLLY JANE!" Pip squealed as he ran.

I stepped into the living room. My eyes popped out a little; I couldn't even help it. Evelyn was pretty scary-looking. She was tall and thin with a really pale face and really black shiny hair. That alone would not have been enough to make her scary; you have to add in the really unhappy face she was wearing. She was also wearing a big black and white striped fur coat that made me think of Cruella De Vil.

"Amelia's not here right now," I said, trying to sound normal. "I'm Molly. I'm taking care of Teddy and Pip."

Evelyn glared at me. Her eyes darted over to the guinea pigs' door and back to me. "When will she be *back*?"

"I don't know."

"I don't suppose you, Margie… Millie, what did you say your name was?"

"Molly. I live next door. I was just watching Teddy and P…"

Evelyn waved her hand around, as if my actual name was not very important, "Molly, then, I don't suppose you… oh, but of *course*." Evelyn grew a big creepy smile on her face. "I see. Oh yes, I see *indeed*. I believe I have solved my little mystery just now."

Solving mysteries is what *I* do. This lady did not look like a detective at all.

"You say you live next door? You are quite friendly with my sister, then?" She made it sound like it was a bad thing to be friendly with her sister.

"Yes. I like Amelia a lot. Don't you?"

"And you seem to have the run of this… *place*, coming here when she's out and attending to the—uh—hamsters and such."

"Actually, they're guinea pigs…"

"She calls us hamsters! She is no good! We fire her!" Teddy squeaked fairly quietly from the next room.

Fortunately, Evelyn was talking too loudly herself so she did not hear him.

"WORST OF TIMES! MOLLY JANE GET HER OUT OF HERE!" Pip screamed.

Again, Angry Evelyn did not even notice.

"I help Amelia and Wally out with lots of things," I said proudly. "They can count on me."

"Uh *huh.*" Evelyn was nodding, still glaring at me. "So, if, for example, my sister was upset and confided in you that she was unhappy about something, let's say, for example, the way the wedding plans were going. You would want to help her, wouldn't you? You would do whatever you could to make her happy, wouldn't you?"

"Sure, if I could. But she never…"

Evelyn said, "Ah ha! Okay, Millie, the game is officially over. I get it. I know what you did." She tossed her heavy handbag onto Amelia's coffee table. It landed with a big thunk and loose things rolled out on top of Amelia's *Brides Today* magazine. "What is this world coming to? This is com*plete*ly out*rag*eous!"

"What are you…? I don't know what you're…"

"Young lady, if Amelia put you up to this, then I suppose it is *less* your fault, but you are, what, twelve years old? Thirteen?"

"Almost ten."

"Whatever. You are old enough to know."

"But I *don't* know…" Good grief, grown-ups can be *so* weird sometimes. What in the world was she talking about?

"And if you did this on your own... well, then, I suggest that you apologize to my sister, quickly and completely, so we can get this all back on track. But don't expect to remain the trusted rodent-sitter and all that comes with it after Amelia finds out what you have done."

Okay, for the record, I am never sassy or disrespectful to grown-ups, even if it seems like they totally deserve it, and she TOTALLY deserved it. But it is so much a part of my training not to smart-off that all I could do was stare at her. I didn't know what it was that I had done and she wasn't telling me. I waited for her to keep talking, hoping and praying that Amelia would come home before I lost my cool and started letting her have it.

"I have done my best to put together this wedding," Evelyn continued, now taking off her black gloves and tossing them angrily on top of the spilled handbag. "Poor little creative-but-unable-to-deal-with-reality-Amelia. Well, if she is so unhappy, then she should certainly have the nerve to tell me *to my face* and not use a little girl like you to let me know. *That* is unacceptable."

"Amelia didn't use me to do anything," I managed to say before she started up again.

"Oh, is that right? So now you are telling me that it was not Amelia's idea—that it was all yours?"

"Ma'am, I don't know what you're talking about. Seriously. Maybe we should call my mom and she can come up and talk to..."

"Oh, you *don't know*, do you? So you are telling me that you did not make a phone call, disguising your voice, pretending to be Amelia, and tell the wedding planner to call everything off because you and Walter are going to *elope*?"

I stared at her. "Why would I..."

"And you did not leave a similar message for me at home, in a ridiculous voice? Are you telling me that Amelia *did this herself*?"

There was a long silence between us. Somewhere a clock ticked and ticked. I could hear Teddy and Pip grumbling and growling softly in the other room.

"There *is* no other explanation. The calls were made on Amelia's cell phone. It was you, acting on your own, or it was you, at her request, or, heaven forbid, it *was* Amelia herself—and that means she has truly lost her nerve, perhaps her very mind, and certainly, my respect as a sister. I am so disgusted."

I was so shocked I couldn't even think of anything to say back to her. I stared stupidly at the woman.

"You don't know anything about this?" Evelyn asked again, her eyes peering into mine.

I shook my head very slowly.

"Well, either you are a really good liar or a really loyal friend, employee or whatever it is that you are to my sister." Evelyn grabbed her gloves and handbag again. She shoved the loose doodads that had fallen out back into it. "You two girls can have a happy time being best friends together. Never mind about Walter and her life as a grown-up... I do not know what has come over that woman. First she abandons her home in the city just when her career is taking off, to live in this *nowhere* suburb in someone's *garage*, for heaven's sake..."

Hey, wait a minute, now, that was just plain mean!

"... and ends up in a relationship with a professor of *Economics* and keeps *hamsters*..." Evelyn continued, making a big huffing sound. "She needed to do this wedding right. The publishers, the media... The PR was going to be perfect for her! Her *people* needed this opportunity to be a part of Amelia Dearling's wedding! It was critical to her career. And *I* had it all put together for her; and now *this*. Millie, do you have any idea how hard I have worked on this wedding?! Have *you* ever planned a wedding? To think that I actually thought, silly me, that I *could* take two days off and do some Christmas shopping... not think about the wedding for a while, do something just for *me*. *"Go ahead, Ev, take two days for yourself, really,"* she says to me, *"...I know that you need time to get ready for your trip to London."* Ha! That is just what she wanted, apparently. For me to be out of touch, just long enough for her to *torpedo everything!* Well, I am through. I am completely through with her and her attitude and her ambivalence. If this is what she wants, then, fine, this is what she can have—nothing. I am through. She has her wish. I will make it come true. You just watch me, Millie."

After saying all of that crazy stuff, Evelyn swept from the room like a furry tornado and slammed the door behind her.

(Hang on, readers; we are time-traveling again! This time back to the present...)

CHAPTER 3 -

Molly to the Rescue

Back to December 22, late afternoon
COUNTDOWN TO CHRISTMAS: 25 24 23 22 21 20 19 18 17

"… and you didn't think that maybe this was something you should *mention* to Amelia? Or to me?" Mom said, her eyes wide. "My goodness, Molly!"

"Mom, I figured if the two of them were having a grown-up type fight, it was none of my business. And if Amelia really did make a phone call with a disguised voice, she'd be kind of… possibly… embarrassed if I brought it up…" my voice trailed off and I shrugged. "I thought maybe it was part of the *Bridezilla* thing."

Amelia's eyes popped open wide and she set her teacup down. This time without spilling. Good job, Amelia.

Mom's mouth was open even wider in some kind of shock. "Molly! For heaven's sake, what did you just say?!"

"It's something that Teddy and Pip said. I'm sorry; I didn't want to say something mean!" I could feel my face getting red.

Mom slumped back into her chair mumbling, "I don't believe this."

But Amelia actually had the tiniest of smiles on her pretty face. "Oh, it's all right, Jane. It isn't something Molly made up herself; Teddy and Pip have given me that lovely nickname as of late. I am not sure where they learned it, it is a fairly clever way to describe a bride planning a big wedding, I suppose. The wedding planning has been very hard on my boys."

"They just feel, you know, like they are getting less attention and stuff," I said to Amelia. "So they are, well mostly *Pip* is, watching a lot of TV, including wedding shows about brides who are… well, you know. They call them *Bridezillas*. The TV show people do. I think maybe it isn't supposed to mean that they are all *that*… bad…" my voice trailed off.

Mom cleared her throat. "But back to the conversation with Evelyn. Molly, she was talking about a phone call made to the wedding planner from Amelia's cell phone, and she thought that *you* had made it. There must be a reason, right?"

"I have no idea why she thought it was me," I said. "She just assumed it was me! It is totally circumstantial. It is the most circumstantial evidence of all evidence. I think."

Circumstantial evidence, in case you don't know, means that… that the evidence is only… like a coincidence. It is not good evidence. It would never hold up in a court of law. Just because I am a girl and the phone call seemed like it was made by a girl, does not prove that the call was made by *me*. It could have been any girl, or any person. Also, Evelyn did not bother to check on my alibi. An alibi is where you were at the time of the crime, instead of doing the crime. Evelyn's case is on thin ice. She is not a good detective. She is not a detective at all.

Amelia was shaking her head. "It's all right. I believe you, Molly," she said quietly. "I have no reason not to believe you. I also believe that Evelyn is… well. I actually don't know what to believe about her. I hardly know what to think about *any* of this. Things were going pretty well, lately. I even told Ev to go ahead and take some time off—to take care of her own business because things were well underway and I thought I could handle anything that came up between then and Christmas…" Amelia twisted her engagement ring around, looked at it, rubbed something off of the diamond, and then sighed again.

"But… something set her off," Mom insisted. "Would Evelyn stop by, all the way from the city, during her time away, and accuse Molly of sabotaging the wedding based on *nothing*? *Some*thing made her believe that Molly was involved."

Amelia and I looked at each other. I had a little thought just then, but it seemed too crazy to mention. It was too circumstantial, or something.

"If it *was* my cell phone…" Amelia mumbled, looking at her diamond again. "I haven't been able to *find* my cell phone, actually, since…" she looked thoughtful. "I can't really remember when I lost it. It was such a relief not to have it ringing all the time."

Speaking of ringing, we were interrupted by the doorbell. I jumped up to answer the door and was relieved to see Wally standing there, his black wool coat dusted with snow, his eyes twinkling. He held out a gloved hand to me. "Molly, Merry Christmas!"

"Wally! Hooray! Come on in," I said, stepping aside. "Boy, am I ever glad to see you! You are just what we needed—a reasonable smart guy. Something crazy is going on and somehow I am right in the middle of it."

Wally raised his eyebrows while nodding his head gravely. "Well, Miss Molly, if nothing else I suppose I *can* provide this situation with the needed 'reasonable guy'. Yes, indeed, it does appear that we have a bit of a mystery on our hands."

"Is everything really cancelled?" I asked, quietly, so Mom and Amelia wouldn't hear in the other room. They had finally gotten calmed down and there was no need to get them both overly excited again. "Did Amelia's sister really do that?"

Wally nodded as he unbuttoned his coat. "I am afraid so. I have tried to contact Evelyn, the wedding planner, the church, the reception hall… it is simply no use."

I took the big heavy coat and laid it across the nearest chair in the dining room. Then I followed him to the living room where he pulled Amelia into a big comforting hug.

"Darling," he said, "are you all right?"

Mom signaled for me to follow her, leaving them alone together. We went into the kitchen. Mom found a bottle of wine and some glasses. "You didn't make those phone calls," she said, kind of quiet, and not looking at me. It wasn't exactly a statement, but not quite a question.

"Mom! I can hardy even believe you're asking me that!" I felt hurt by all of the lack of faith she was showing in me.

Mom saw the look on my face and softened up right away. "Oh, I'm so sorry, Molly," she said, putting down glasses and pulling me into a hug. "This is all so very strange. And I hate to think that Amelia is the one who… but…"

She stopped talking because she heard Wally calling us from the other room, apologizing for chasing us out.

"We have finished with our *mushy* moment, it is safe to return!" he called cheerily.

We returned with the wine and glasses. I jabbed a straw into a juice box. I had wanted to squeeze the juice into a fancy wine glass, but Mom said it would just make a mess and most of it would end up on the counter and… you know the drill.

"Jane, thank you," Wally said, taking the glass of wine that Mom offered. "We do appreciate all that you are doing. And your home is so festive and warm, so welcoming. It is a pleasure to be here."

Mom looked very happy about that. Wally always said things that made my mom grinny and happy. She handed another glass to Amelia who kind of gulped it down. "You and Amelia are always welcome here," Mom said. "You know that. You are family. Whatever we can do for you, you know we will do it."

"I got here as quickly as I could, what with the weather and traffic and all," Wally said, setting his glass down on the coffee table, just as Mom slipped a coaster under it. ('Super Mom— Protector of Fine Wood Furniture!') "I was at my desk, finishing some grading, when my phone rang and it was Evelyn, who is not generally in the habit of speaking to me much less calling me at my office."

Amelia looked apologetically at Wally.

"She told me that she had tried to reach Amelia several times, had left messages and gotten no reply. Since the home phone is unlisted—and apparently is not shared with Evelyn—she became desperate and called me." Wally took a sip of his wine.

Amelia sighed and sat back against the cushions, rubbing her temples.

"Her main purpose in calling was not to converse, but rather to convey to me that she had cancelled the wedding, in its entirety, and was leaving for London. I was in a bit of shock and was unable to formulate any helpful questions before she hung up on me. I'm afraid I don't have much more to add."

We all kind of slumped and sighed. We had been hoping that Wally would have more to tell us than that.

Then Wally sat up straighter, "Molly, you are the detective here. Perhaps with your help, we can look at some of the clues before us and figure out what is going on."

I nodded eagerly. 'Molly to the rescue' was a whole lot better than 'Molly in the interrogation chair'.

"Evelyn believes that you, or Amelia, made phone calls from Amelia's cell phone in order to call off the wedding. She is basing this belief on circumstantial evidence of course…"

"Exactly!" I said.

"…but *strong* evidence, unfortunately, as the calls apparently *were* made from Amelia's cell phone. Let's talk about motive and opportunity."

Mom looked kind of freaked out by the way the conversation was going, but she settled back in her chair and sipped her wine without saying anything.

"I, of course, had opportunity," Amelia said softly. "But it wasn't me. Motive? How I am, or was, feeling about the wedding is, well, it's all strangely separate from this conversation."

Wally looked at her curiously, and then turned to me.

"Me? I guess I had some opportunities," I admitted. "Only because I spent time around Amelia and at the apartment—so I could help out with Teddy and Pip. But I wouldn't have had a chance to use her cell phone; she always had it with her. Besides, I didn't have *any* motive. I want you guys to get married! I helped you two get together, remember? I totally want the wedding to work out! The ones who aren't too happy about it are Teddy and Pip."

(Fasten your seatbelts again, readers, we are going to do some more of that backwards time-traveling so we can relive my memory. Are you ready? Let's go!)

CHAPTER 4 -

Shh!

Back to December 17, evening
COUNTDOWN TO CHRISTMAS: 25 24 23 22 21 20 19 18 **17**

"You are an *angel*, Molly, my guardian angel! Thank you so much for coming!" Amelia said, ushering me into the tiny apartment and taking my coat. I slipped off my boots and left them to drip on a mat by the door. "If you could talk to them, keep them quiet, something, *any*thing, I would be *so* appreciative. I will be right there, in my room. I believe with that door closed, their door closed, and your calming influence, I may be able to get through these few phone calls…"

"How's all the wedding stuff going?" I asked, noticing Amelia's less than happy smile. I had always thought that brides were supposed to be happy. Amelia looked totally stressed out.

"Oh, Molly," Amelia sighed. "…let me give you some advice to tuck away for twenty or so years from now when you are a bride-to-be… elope."

I made a face.

"That means to run away somewhere and have a private ceremony."

I shook my head. "Thanks for the advice, but I'm not getting married. Ever."

She nodded. "No, of course not. I understand. I wasn't ever planning on it, either, really, until just recently..." Amelia's cell phone started ringing. Her ring tone, *Here Comes the Bride*, tinkled out softly. It was cute and funny, at least it was to me. Amelia didn't smile about it. She actually looked irritated and answered with a quick. "Yes? Oh hi, Sunny..." Then she mouthed the words "thank you" to me and disappeared into her bedroom, closing the door quietly behind her.

I could hear Teddy and Pip, behind their closed door, making quite a lot of noise. I remembered the very first time we'd met and how much squealing they had done. I had to cover my ears, and Daddy had made an excuse to leave the whole entire apartment. They weren't exactly that noisy now. They were noisier. The TV was on really loud and Pip was yelling, or maybe singing, I couldn't tell which. It also sounded like things were being knocked around. I opened the door and closed it behind me really fast.

"Hello? Teddy? Pip? It's me, Molly."

It was quiet for about one second, and then they both came running from wherever they had been to be as close to me as possible, calling my name over and over again.

"Molly Jane!"

"MOLLY JANE!"

"Molly Jane is here to see her best friends! Molly Jane where have you BEEN for all of these days and days!?"

"MOLLY JANE! MOLLY JANE! MOLLY JANE! BEST FRIEND MOLLY JANE!"

I reached out and pet them both. They pushed at each other trying to be closest to my hand. I tried petting with both hands at once.

"Hey, Pip, honey, could you turn off the TV for a little while, huh?" I said loudly, nodding my head at the big TV that was blaring a cartoon.

"PIP LIKES TV AND HE LIKES IT LOUD! But Pip will quiet it for Molly Jane." Pip caught a look from Teddy and raced off to the far corner of their wonderfully large living space and pushed the mute button on the remote with his little front paw.

It was nice and quiet for another few seconds, until I asked, "How's it going?"

You know how sometimes a person will just say "fine" when you ask that question? What I got was an incredible amount of guinea-pig-style complaints and comments in such a jumble; I could hardly make it all out. It went something like this:

Me: "Hey, you guys, shhh! Okay? Amelia is trying to…"

Pip: *"Shhh is NO GOOD! WE ARE TIRED OF HEARING THAT THING!"*

Me: "Amelia asked me to come up here and keep you company…"

Teddy, with a sigh: *"Amelia asks Molly Jane to come here to "shhh!" at us and it is no good. That is the fact of that matter."*

Pip: *"Matters are NO GOOD!"*

Me: "Amelia needs to make some phone calls, so she needs you to stay a little more quiet while she…"

Teddy: *"Amelia is talking on her sell phone too much of the times! Amelia is Bridezilla now. We are much afraid."*

Pip: *"NO GOOD!"*

Teddy: *"We have no more patience for the phone-talking and want much attention from best friends!"*

Me: "Um…"

Teddy: *"And one time, not so long ago, Amelia was gone from here for very long and it was dark outside and there was never even dinner for the best friends. And there was no Molly Jane to come and feed us so we had to have Mom Jane come here which is…"*

Pip: *"NO GOOD! WORST OF TIMES! WE FIRED MOM JANE, SHE SHOULD NOT BE BACK!"*

Me: "Yeah, I know, I'm sorry about that day. I really wanted to come up, but I had a Girl Scout meeting to go to and..."

Teddy: *"Squirrel Snouts? What is that thing?! It sounds no good. Always Molly Jane has that thing! Squirrels do not even have those things called snouts."*

Pip: *"OBJECTION!"*

Me (giggling): "Not Squirrel Snouts, guys, Girl Scouts—and I only have meetings twice a month..."

Pip: *"Twice a month is TOO MUCH! WORST OF TIMES!"*

Teddy: *"What means Girl Scouts anyway, Molly Jane? It still sounds no good. Why do girls need to do the scouting anyway? That sounds like grown-up work for big men. Dangerous and not good."*

Pip: *"MOLLY JANE SHOULD STAY HOME AND PLAY WITH BEST FRIENDS TEDDY AND PIP!"*

Me: "We do fun things like making crafts..."

Pip: *"CRAFTS ARE NO GOOD!"*

Me: "... and playing games, earning badges... and stuff."

Pip: *"BADGERS ARE NO GOOD! STUFF IS NO GOOD!"*

Teddy: *"Why does Molly Jane have to do the crafts and game play every single one of the days?"*

Me: "Teddy, honey, it's only two times a month. That means 28 or 29 days in a month that I don't do it."

Silence.

Pip: *"CRAFTS ARE NO GOOD! MAX IS NO GOOD! MOM JANE..."*

Me: "Wow! Guys, you are really upset. I don't think it's because of my Girl Scout meetings. Do you want to tell me what's really bothering you? Maybe I could help."

Silence.

Teddy: "*We are neglected.*"

Pip: "*AMELIA IS BRIDEZILLA; SHE HAS TURNED INTO A MONSTER!*"

Teddy: "*Amelia is only best friends with Wedding Planner these days. And no-good sister the name of Evelyn. Amelia has turned into the monster of Bridezilla. And Molly Jane is too busy with her fourth grade homework and Squirrel Snouts. Wally is afraid of wedding plans so he stays at his Princeton and makes extra homework for his sleepy kids. We want attention.*"

Pip: "*NO ATTENTION IS NOT ENOUGH!*"

Teddy: "*Pip watches TV very too much of the day and is learning about courtroom drama as well as real estate tips. And wedding planning. There is the show of Bridezillas, it is much much scary.*"

Pip, quietly: "*Pip is smarter than ever, but still things are no good.*"

Me: "Oh, sweeties, I'm so sorry…"

Teddy: "*Always people are so sorry—but never do things get better for Teddy and Pip.*"

Pip: "*WE OBJECT!*"

Teddy: "*Objection sustained, Pip.*"

Pip: "*The defense rests. Next case.*"

Me: "Have you talked to Amelia or Wally about this?"

Teddy: "*We talk and talk and squeal and scream and wheek—and still there is no listening. Only door-closing and "shh"ing and sending over of Molly Jane to "shh" at us more.*"

Pip: "*AND WE OBJECT!*"

Teddy: "*Our feelings are hurting and our nerves are being stood on and we are... upset.*"

The door opened and Amelia walked into the room with a tired smile on her face. "Thank you, Molly; I think we can call it a night."

"It's okay, I can stay a while…"

Amelia shook her head. "You should get back to your homework. You have done so much, and we are grateful."

"Did my mom call you? I really don't have that much homework to do…"

Amelia just smiled. "Say goodnight, boys!"

"MOLLY JANE SHOULD STAY! WORST OF TIMES! OBJECTION!"

"Good night guys!" I gave them each a gentle pat on the head, and followed Amelia out of the room. "I guess I need to go."

"I'll walk you home, Molly, it's the least I can do; it's so dark out there…" Amelia hesitated before she picked up her coat. "Could I ask you something?"

I nodded as I wrestled with the zipper on my own coat.

"Let's say, just pretending, that it is *your* wedding that you have to plan. What kind of a wedding would you put together?"

I frowned a little, thinking hard about that question. "Well…" It was so hard to say since I wasn't going to ever get married and hadn't ever thought about it.

"What comes to your mind right away—without think-ing too hard?" Amelia asked, not giving me much time to let any thoughts come into my mind at all.

"Well… I think maybe my wedding shouldn't be a big deal, because it would be too expensive, and Daddy would have to pay for it. And it seems like it can be a big pain in the… in the *something* to plan it all. So I'd make it simple. And I'd make it on Christmas Eve; that would be cool. But I'd have the most awesome dress—that part would be important. Daddy would pay for that part with no complaining."

Amelia smiled at me, nodding. "Of course he would."

"I think a wedding should probably be kind of like matching the person. You know, like, if you're a person who likes horses, it should be at a ranch, or you should ride a horse. Stuff like that. Like, it would be kind of dumb to ride on a horse if you totally don't like horses, or are afraid of them... but if you're marrying someone who likes horses, then... you should have them be part of it, but don't ride one, because you shouldn't be terrified about stuff on the wedding day. But maybe people who don't both like horses together shouldn't get married in the first place. I guess I would have to have guinea pigs in my wedding. I love guinea pigs." I shrugged. "I wouldn't marry any person who didn't like guinea pigs."

Amelia surprised me then and gave me a big hug. "Oh, Molly, you are such a wise person. Are you sure you're only nine years old?"

"Almost ten," I said, looking at her curiously. "Are you okay, Amelia?"

Amelia gave herself a shake and forced a big smile, but I could see that she had shiny eyes, teary eyes. "Yes. Great. Now, let's get you home."

We walked down the stairs and out into the snowy backyard without saying much more. I wondered about Amelia's questions, but didn't think I should bug her with my own. Grown-ups can be mysterious, but this was not a mystery I felt like I should be trying to solve.

"Call me again if you need someone to talk to the guys!" I said, as we said goodnight at my back door.

"I certainly will," Amelia promised. "Good night Miss Molly. And thank you."

Mom was wrapping a Christmas present at the kitchen table. "Is that for me?" I asked, tossing my coat over the back of a chair. It didn't quite stick and slumped onto the floor.

Mom nodded her head at the coat on the floor. She didn't answer my question. She was humming *Jingle Bells*.

"I think Amelia needs someone to talk to about her wedding," I said, tossing the coat onto the chair. This time it stayed put.

Mom stopped humming and wrapping and looked at me. "Coat. Closet," she said.

"She tried to talk to me about it, but I wasn't much help," I said, eyeing the mostly-wrapped package with detective-eyes, wondering what it was. I wrestled my coat onto a hook in the closet.

"Really?" Mom said, raising her eyebrows a little. "I hope everything is all right."

"Teddy and Pip were complaining that Amelia hasn't been paying enough attention to them lately," I continued. "They said even Wally is staying away. That seems kind of all mixed up to me."

At the mention of Teddy and Pip, Mom went back to her wrapping. In spite of their total coolness and cuteness, Mom does not really like Teddy and Pip. The feeing is very mutual.

"That's how it gets with weddings," she said quietly. "... at least it seems like that's the way it gets these days, I mean. When your dad and I were... well, we didn't have much money and our ideas weren't so elaborate. But even that was kind of stressful. You try to please everyone and forget that the most important thing is that you're *marrying* someone."

I frowned at that. "Sounds crazy to me. To forget that you're marrying someone."

Mom grinned at me. "I didn't mean that *literally*, silly."

"You and Daddy don't have to worry. My wedding will be simple and cheap, except for the dress. But I'm not getting married anyway, so never mind."

"Okey dokey, Mol," Mom said. "Now, how about you finish that homework."

(That is the end of my flashback... get ready to go back to the present, okay readers?)

CHAPTER 5 -

Clue Finding

Back to December 22, late afternoon

*COUNTDOWN TO CHRISTMAS: 25 24 23 **22** 21 20 19 18 17*

Amelia sighed. "I know. I know how upset they've been. I guess I only really paid attention to how incredibly... difficult they've been. I was only thinking about myself."

Wally chuckled softly, "Amelia, darling, really, it is quite understandable if you did not put the guinea pigs' needs above your own while seeing to the wedding."

I could hear Mom mumbling her agreement at that.

"But they gave me so many clues. I should have paid more attention," Amelia said sadly.

Mom cleared her throat and said, "Aren't we possibly getting a little bit off track, maybe? Weren't we trying to figure out why Evelyn thought you had wanted to cancel the wedding?"

Amelia nodded. "I did try to tell her something one night. Perhaps it was the very next night, after Molly had come by. I was going to bravely attempt to shift things around a bit. Evelyn can be quite a force, you see, and she had taken things over almost completely. I *was* unhappy at that point, I will admit it, with the direction things were going..."

(This time, we are backwards time-traveling to Amelia's memory. Are you ready? Let's go!)

CHAPTER 6 -

Standing up to Evelyn

Back to December 18, evening
*COUNTDOWN TO CHRISTMAS: 25 24 23 22 21 20 19 **18** 17*
    "I have asked you to come by tonight," Amelia began, and then had to clear her throat, because she was so nervous. Her voice was coming out higher and very different than her usual smooth calm style. "Because we need to talk seriously about the direction the wedding is taking. I do appreciate... all that you have done, and are doing, and... it maybe just isn't exactly, well, *me*. The wedding isn't exactly me. And I was thinking..."
    Nearby, Teddy and Pip were setting an all-time record for noisiness. They had promised Amelia that they would not do any talking while Evelyn and Sunny were in the apartment, as neither knew about this carefully guarded secret. They had not, however, promised to be quiet.
    "Excuse me," Amelia said quietly, and slipped into the guinea pigs' room.
    The guinea pigs looked up at her expectantly, quietly, side by side. But Amelia did not speak to them; she merely removed the TV remote control from their reach, turned off the television, and returned to her meeting, closing the door behind her.

Evelyn, Amelia's older sister, was frowning toward the closed door of the guinea pigs' room, and Sunny, the wedding planner, was checking her watch and bouncing her knee impatiently. The meeting had only just started, but it was not going well at all.

The lack of TV did not seem to have made enough difference. The noise from Teddy and Pip's room was still very distracting.

"I am so sorry; excuse me for a moment," Amelia said, leaving the room again, and going into Teddy and Pip's room. She closed their door and walked up to them, speaking softly as they quieted down to listen. "Darlings, seriously, if you care for me at *all*…"

"Amelia is having a Best Friends Club meeting without us and we are unhappy," Teddy squeaked quietly. *"These are the worst of times. You are doing the no-good thing of neglecting us. We will not be quiet until the no-good ladies are gone."*

Amelia looked from Teddy to Pip, who was nodding his agreement from the upper ramp, having just knocked over his igloo, which banged noisily against the wall. "Please," Amelia began. "I need to talk to them, just for tonight. After this, it will be better, I know it will."

"We are some sorry, Amelia, best friend, but we are doing the thing of taking a stand," Teddy said firmly. *"This is no good and you must do what we say and want. The end."*

"The end!" Pip squeaked his agreement.

THE SAME NIGHT… A LITTLE WHILE LATER…
"Hello, Jane… I simply cannot believe I am asking this of you, but is Molly home? I need a *really* big favor."

(Hi readers, it's Molly! Get ready because we are going to go back to the present…)

CHAPTER 7 -
Still Clue Finding

Back to December 22, late afternoon
*COUNTDOWN TO CHRISTMAS: 25 24 23 **22** 21 20 19 18 17*

"Oh yeah, that was the night you brought them over to our house!" I said. "We had a talk then, about how they were feeling…"

"Back to the guinea pigs..." Mom muttered.

(Backwards time-traveling to my memory. Are you ready? Let's go!)

CHAPTER 8 –

Molly Jane's Christmas House

Back to December 18, same evening
*COUNTDOWN TO CHRISTMAS: 25 24 23 22 21 20 19 **18** 17*

Amelia stood in our kitchen, snow melting off of her coat and dripping onto the floor, holding two boxes. One of them, covered with a purple quilt, was squeaking and squirming. Amelia looked anxiously at my mom.

"Uh…" was all that Mom could manage before I spoke up.

"Are Teddy and Pip in there? Can I see them? Don't worry; I am so happy to babysit for you!" I pulled back the quilt to peek at the guinea pigs.

Amelia, looking really relieved, set the squirming box on the kitchen table and the other box on the floor. "Molly, I do apologize for this, it's so sudden and such an imposition, after you just helped me last night, I know…"

"It *totally* isn't!" I interrupted. "Hi guys! Welcome to my house! Isn't this fun?" I said, looking down at my two favorite guinea pigs. They did not look as happy as I would have thought.

"It's fine, Amelia," I heard Mom saying, though I could tell she didn't really mean it. "We will look after them. When… when do you think you'll be *back* to get them?"

"Not more than an hour, I promise," Amelia said, glancing at her watch. "You see, I'm having a wedding planning gathering at the apartment. My sister is there, and Sunny, the wedding planner. The boys..." she lowered her voice. "...were causing *such* a ruckus! I honestly didn't know what to do—even with their door closed we simply could not hear each other talk. It is so unlike them; I really don't know what has gotten into them. Well, at any rate, I will be back to fetch them as soon as possible. They don't need a thing; just keep an eye on them." Amelia smiled at Mom. "Oh, and this is their litter box for, well, *you know*. They are *very* good about only *going* in there."

Mom opened her mouth to ask a question, but Amelia was already dashing through the snow back to the apartment. I heard Mom let out a big heavy sigh before she turned to look at me. The guinea pigs, who hadn't made a sound, just stood there in the box looking up at me and glancing out of the corner of their little eyes at my mom.

"You still have to get your homework done," Mom finally said. "And practice your piano."

"I can't believe I have homework this close to Christmas," I grumbled. "I know! Teddy and Pip can help me! Right guys?"

Teddy and Pip stared at me for a few seconds.

"HOMEWORK IS NO GOOD! PIANO IS NO GOOD!" Pip shouted in his squeaky yelling way, then turned to glare at Mom.

"Molly Jane, we will help you with anything you say," Teddy said apologetically. *"Pip is not doing manners today. Hi Mom Jane, nice day?"*

"I'll be keeping an eye on *all* of you," Mom said, giving me a slight smile and heading out of the kitchen. "Homework, Molly. And they had better use that litter box thingy for *you know*."

"MOM JANE IS NO GOOD!" squealed Pip, who had begun to attempt an escape from the box without any success. *"I WILL DO MY POTTY WHERE I WANT!"*

"Pip does not mean that thing," Teddy assured me. *"He is bad-manners today but will not do that bad thing."*

"Well, that's a relief. I have my stuff all laid out in the living room. Let's go in there. Now promise me, guys, that you will stay right by me, no funny business, okay? Or I'll have to put you back in that box... or something." I only said that part so Mom would hear, but then whispered close to their ears, "I wouldn't really do that. Just be good, okay?"

"Pip will be good," Pip said with a sigh. *"Close to Molly Jane will be Pip. No potty on Mom Jane's floor. But being good is no good."*

I set Pip down next to my backpack then reached into the box to get Teddy. As I set Teddy down, I noticed that Pip hadn't moved an inch. He was staring at our Christmas tree with his little mouth hanging open. The lights were on and it was really pretty. We had done a great job on the decorating this year. Teddy, too, stared at the Christmas tree with his little mouth hanging open.

"Molly Jane? Is now the time of... Christmas?" Teddy asked quietly. *"Maybe Molly Jane's family does a tree for not Christmas? Is this a Thanksgiving Tree?"*

"Um," I pet his little head gently. "Didn't you know...?"

"There is no Christmas at our house," Pip said. *"Our house is no good. There is no Christmas."* Then Pip sang a little song:

> *There is no Christmas – at our house*
> *There are no lights and no tree*
> *There is no Christmas – at our house*
> *No Christmas for Teddy and me*
>
> *There is no Christmas - at our house*
> *No presents or stockings to see*
> *There is no Christmas - at our house*
> *We want to come live with Mol-ly."*

"Oh Pip... I am so sorry honey. I didn't even notice yesterday... I'm sorry guys. Of course you're upset by that. You know... it's probably because... it's just that... I mean Amelia and Wally are..." I sighed and pet them each gently for a while. "I don't know, I guess," I finally said, "but we *can* enjoy Christmas here, tonight, okay? I'll put on some music and you guys can look at the tree and other pretty things while I start my homework."

"Amelia is the 'Grinch who Stole our Christmas'. Except she is not green," Pip said.

"Oh, Pip..." I tried to pet his head but he backed away.

"Amelia is 'Bridezilla, the Grinch Who is not Being a Best Friend'."

"Amelia is just *so* busy and running behind schedule," I offered.

"BUSY IS NO GOOD! WEDDING IS NO GOOD! STUFF IS NO GOOD!" Pip squealed.

"Molly? Are you doing your homework?" Came Mom's voice from somewhere in the house.

"AND MOM JANE IS NO GOOD!" Pip stamped a little paw.

"You bet!" I answered Mom, finding my place on the vocabulary worksheet and grabbing a pencil. "I know you are upset, but, guys, I need to do some homework. Help me think of a sentence that uses the word *regular*. Then we can talk more, okay?"

"Regular is no good. Amelia is 'The Grinch who Stole Christmas from Best Friends Pip and Teddy'."

"Thanks Pip. That's a good and really long sentence."

Teddy wandered over to where my pencil was scratching away on my paper and tried to chew on it. *"Molly Jane, homework is truly no fun. Let's play."*

"HOMEWORK IS NO GOOD! WRITING IS NO GOOD!" Pip shouted—right into my ear.

I rubbed at my ear and said, "Come on, Pip, writing *is* good, Amelia is a writer."

"Amelia is not so much writing these days," Teddy said. *"She is only planning a wedding. Amelia is taking a no-good break from being Amelia,"* he added wisely. *"Now even our Wally is not so much around. We think Wally is afraid of the Bridezilla."*

"Molly?" There was Mom again.

"We have *so* much to talk about… and I promise we will. I just have to do a few more things…"

"Now Molly Jane sounds like our Amelia too," Teddy sighed. *"Bridezilla is a bad thing and Molly Jane catches it from Amelia. Why is there no Christmas at our house?"* Teddy asked. *"Never before has Amelia or Wally not had Christmas for their best friends Teddy and Pip. Are we not good? Did we start being no good?"*

"Oh, honey, of course that's not it!" I said, petting him reassuringly. I could feel Pip starting to climb up my sweater and onto my back. "… but she did say that you were making so much noise over there that they couldn't have their meeting…"

"That was only just Pip," Teddy said quickly. *"Only Pip does that no-good thing."*

"Teddy is a no-good tattle-tale," Pip squeaked. He had found his way to the back of my neck and it tickled like crazy. I had to twist one arm around my back to try to pick him up; it was not easy because I am not flexible like a circus performer, you know.

"Teddy, Pip, how about this. Let me write a few sentences and then we can talk, okay? I promise you will have my full attention. Now, the word regular… let's see… how about this: My friends' lives have not been regular since the wedding plans started."

"True," Teddy nodded. *"Good work, Molly Jane. You have a star on your paper from Teddy."*

We struggled through a bunch of sentences.

Guinea Pig Suggestions:

1. Communication is no good, it is the worst of times.
2. I would like a treat.
3. Friendship is no good when there is no Christmas.
4. Evaluation is no good and I don't know what that thing even is.
5. Where is my treat, Molly Jane?
6. Nationality is no good when the Grinch steals your Christmas.

It turned out that I had to come up with my own sentences. So much for getting Teddy and Pip to help me. But eventually, I was able to pack up the papers and call it 'done'.

"Molly, don't forget to practice your piano!" Mom called. "You gave me your word."

"Okay!" I answered. "Come on guys, let's go over by the piano and I'll play you some Christmas songs."

I started with Jingle Bells. Pip sang along, making up some less than festive words:

Jingle bells
Christmas smells
Weddings are no good.
Wally never visits us
And Amelia is the Bridezilla... who stole our CHRIST-
MAS!

"*Molly Jane, piano practice is more fun than homework, but not much,*" Pip sighed quietly.

"Okay, you two, what's going on?" I asked. Both guinea pigs were in my lap now. Teddy purring happily, looking at the Christmas tree, Pip still grumbling and muttering under his breath.

"*Can we live here with Molly Jane? Where it is Christmas?*" Teddy asked, looking up at me with his sweet little eyes.

"*Amelia is Bridezilla,*" Pip said, still grumpy. "*Best friend Amelia is gone and we are stuck with only a bride monster who talks always on her celery phone and who does not do Christmas."*

"I can't believe Amelia is being like that," I said. "She's a quiet writer, and doesn't even like to talk on the phone."

"Amelia is not much of Amelia these days," Teddy said. *"She talks MUCH on the tellyphone and sell phone. Always that no-good sister is around. Amelia gets mad about things that before would not make a difference to herself. It is much confusing."*

"WE NEED A PLAN! MOLLY JANE CALL MAX AND SAVE THE DAY!" Pip suddenly sat up and shouted. *"THAT'S IT! HOORAY! Plus I would like a treat."*

"I wish I could help you, but what am I supposed to exactly, do?"

Pip stared at me.

"I mean, it's not like there's a mystery to solve, right? You guys are just upset because Amelia is all caught-up in her wedding plans. I can't do much about that."

"Molly Jane can steal the wedding. Like the Grinch Stealing Christmas!" Teddy said excitedly. *"That idea would work!"*

I didn't know what to say about that. I smiled at their expectant little faces and pet them both. But when I hadn't responded in a while, Pip started shouting again.

"MOLLY JANE IS NOT HELPING! PIP WILL HAVE TO SAVE THE DAY ALL BY HIMSELF! Molly Jane, Pip needs to do his potty."

I let Pip down so he could run to the covered litter box. "Pip, you know I would do anything I could, don't you? I love you guys. But I can't do something like stop a wedding. Do you know how much trouble I'd be in? I'd never get to see you guys again! Besides, Amelia and Wally want to get married. Why would we want to stop them? Remember this summer when we all worked so hard to get them to stay together? And, finally, I can't think of anything that I could do that would work anyway."

"FIRE WEDDING PLANNER! SHE IS NO GOOD!" I heard Pip shouting. It was muffled because he was inside the litter box. *"MOLLY JANE CAN DO IT! SHE IS AT OUR HOUSE RIGHT NOW, GO MOLLY JANE GO!"*

"Well…"

"THEN FIRE NO-GOOD SISTER EVELYN—SHE NEEDS TO BE FIRED AND GO BACK TO BIG CITY WHERE SHE WILL NOT PINCH HER NOSE AND SAY MEAN THINGS ABOUT GUINEA PIGS! SHE IS AT OUR HOUSE TOO, FIRE THEM BOTH WITH ONE BIG FLAME!"

"Amelia's sister doesn't like guinea pigs?"

"Evelyn is a person called a snob," Teddy said. *"She does not have liking for animals of any sort. Unless she is wearing their fur as a coat. We are afraid she is wanting to make a coat out of Teddy and his Pip."*

"NO GOOD! OBJECTION! SUSTAINED! CASE CLOSED! BAILIFF—TAKE HER AWAY!" Pip screamed.

This talk was new. I looked at Teddy.

"Pip finds Court TV show and learns courtroom talk. It is his new Pip-thing." Teddy shrugged. *"It is just Pip. I cannot explain him."*

Pip was back and trying to climb up my leg. I picked him up and put him in my lap again.

"MOLLY JANE! WHY IS THAT NO-GOOD THING IN YOUR CHRISTMAS HOUSE?" Pip suddenly screamed. I turned to look where his eyes were focused and saw Mom's cell phone on the coffee table.

"It's okay, it's only Mom's phone," I said softly.

"It is the sell phone that makes our Amelia so unhappy," Teddy said. *"Always when she is talking into it or listening from it, she has a frowny face. And also, she is not spending the moments with best friends Teddy and Pip."*

I pet him for a while and tried to say reassuring things. "I don't think it's the phone, really, it's what the people are talking about that's making her frown, don't you think?"

"CELERY PHONE IS NO GOOD! WORST OF TIMES!" Pip screamed. *"IT IS A NO-GOOD THING, MUCH BAD, PLEASE TAKE IT AWAY AND THROW IT IN THE GARBAGE RIGHT NOW MOLLY JANE! Thank you. Plus, I would like a treat. You are ignoring my asking for a treat many times!"*

I set the guinea pigs down and went to the kitchen where I found a container with leftover salad in it from dinner. I put a few pieces of lettuce on a napkin and brought it into the living room for the guys. They ate it in about two seconds and wanted more.

"MOLLY JANE! DO NOT FORGET! YOU NEED TO THROW THAT CELERY PHONE INTO THE GARBAGE!" Pip yelled.

I reached over and picked up Mom's phone. Both guinea pigs backed away from it. "Look, you guys, it's not bad; it's just a little machine. Take a look, don't worry, I'm holding it."

At this, they both edged toward the phone very slowly, then sniffed at it, backed away quickly, then edged forward again.

"No good," Pip whispered.

I could tell that he was fascinated by it. "This is how it works," I said, opening it up. "See this screen? It will show a number or a picture of who is calling. And the phone can ring different ways for different calls. It's really cool."

"No good," Pip said again, but still stared at the cell phone, climbing over my hand to get a closer look.

"You can take pictures with it, too, see?" I said, holding it up and snapping a picture of Pip. I showed it to him.

"TEDDY! LOOK! PIP IS ME AND I AM ON THE CELERY PHONE! But still it is a no-good thing that needs to be stomped on and put into the garbage and then crushed up by the

garbage-disposer and tossed into the big green truck and taken away to a big dump somewhere far far away." Pip turned his back on the cell phone, but kept turning slightly to take peeks.

Teddy nosed his way closer so he could see.

"Molly Jane, take a picture of me, it is no fair that Pip is on this phone and not Teddy who is the boss of the guinea pigs."

I snapped a picture of Teddy, too, and showed it to him.

"Molly Jane, you could make your movies with the sell phone and save the day!" Teddy suggested. *"What do you think of my idea?"*

"Well…"

"How is there talking with these sell phones? Is it like walkie-talkie that we have at our house to talk to Molly Jane in her house?" Teddy wanted to know.

I opened the phone again and hit the *send* button. "On this phone, you can choose a button and push it and it dials up someone. The last phone call my mom made was to my dad…"

"MOM JANE IS NO GOOD!" Pip squeaked, taking another peek at the phone.

I ignored that. "If I wanted to call someone else, I would push on this button until it was on a number I wanted… or you can just push in the numbers…"

"PIP WANTS TO TRY!" Suddenly, Pip was not only facing Mom's phone, he was standing on it, stomping on buttons with his little feet.

"Hey, cool it!" I giggled. "I don't think you need to be using a cell phone right now."

"Someday, Molly Jane, you can teach us how to do this thing and we can do walkie-talkie with you, okay?" Teddy said, and then did a cute little guinea pig yawn. *"Maybe. Someday."* He sounded really sad when he said that.

"You guys, the thing about the wedding and all that is, well, Amelia is probably having a really hard time being in the middle of it all," I said reasonably. "She has to be nice to those two ladies but also try to keep you guys happy."

"*Amelia is not doing a good job. We feel she is not in any middle, she is on the side of the bad people, not her best friends,*" Teddy said.

"*WORST OF TIMES! WE OBJECT! CASE CLOSED!*" Pip yelled.

Mom walked in, her mouth opened to say something, but then she just shook her head and walked back out. She is not used to the fact that these guinea pigs can talk. I think she would rather not hear it at all.

"Have you tried talking to Amelia yet?"

"*Of course, Molly Jane. Always we are talking. We talk and talk—and talk and talk to Amelia—but Amelia is not hearing us.*"

I sighed. I couldn't think of anything I could say that would make these two feel better. Telling them that it would only be a few more weeks would not help at all. To a guinea pig, time is totally different. Waiting is not something they are good at. They have a hard time looking past a single day.

Pip started singing a little song very quietly:

Amelia, Amelia, oh how I miss Amelia.
The wedding is no good.
Wedding Planner is no good.
Oh how I miss Amelia.

"*Molly Jane—we have not even told you of the worst thing,*" Teddy said. "*Pip and me, we do not like to speak of it. But since we have already spilled all of our beans to you, we might as well tell you this bad part too.*"

"Okay, what is it?" I suddenly felt really nervous.

"*Amelia is getting phone calls from realtors,*" Teddy said. "*Realtor means moving... away.*"

"*HGTV,*" Pip said quietly, nodding his head. "*Times cannot be worse. I object.*"

(Ready to go back to the present? Hang on guys, here we go....)

CHAPTER 9 -

Moving?

Back to December 22, late afternoon
COUNTDOWN TO CHRISTMAS: 25 24 23 **22** *21 20 19 18 17*

"Oh dear," Amelia said. "Oh dear! I did not realize that they had overheard that message…"

"Darling? Are you… were you discussing matters with realtors?" Wally looked a little surprised and shocked.

"Oh, Wally, no, not at all. I would never do something like that without discussing it first with you. I simply allowed Evelyn to tell one of her many realtors to call me. I only did that so she would stop badgering me. I had no intention of doing anything. Surely the message mentioned properties in Manhattan… oh the poor little dears! I am sure they were completely worried when they heard that message."

"So you aren't really thinking about moving back to the city?" I asked, crossing my fingers.

Amelia shook her head. "I haven't had a chance to think about such a thing, and, honestly, I…" She looked at Wally. "I don't want that. Do you?"

Wally gave his head a little shake. "I want to be with you, Amelia, wher*ever* that may be."

"Yay!" I shouted, clapping my hands together. "Then you guys can just always stay here!"

Mom gave me a look, but Amelia and Wally just laughed. It was nice to see them laughing. Amelia wasn't looking sad at all anymore.

"We have no plans. We haven't discussed where we will be living much at all," Amelia admitted. "I love the apartment, though and I expect that we will be there a while. At least until we decide that something else is needed. I promise that any serious ideas about moving will be shared with the Fisher family. Okay?"

I nodded, but I felt kind of sad again, because 'a while' was hardly the same as forever.

"And, most likely, any moving at all would be right here within this area, so we could stay close to you. You are like family to me."

"And to me," Wally added.

"We feel the same," Mom said, smiling at them both.

I settled back in my chair, feeling like nothing else mattered, and it didn't to me. They weren't leaving. So what if the wedding was called off? Big deal! They could plan a different one.

Amelia started to laugh, softly, then more loudly. "Oh my goodness!" she finally said. "I cannot believe that I have reduced myself to *'The Bridezilla Who Stole Christmas!'* How did this all happen?" She leaned on Wally's shoulder, still laughing a little bit crazily. "My poor Teddy and Pip. Thinking we were moving, and missing Christmas…"

"But Daddy and I brought over some Christmas for them yesterday. I thought that really helped," I said. "I mean, I think Teddy and Pip were feeling much better by the time we left."

"I suppose. But they were so very upset before that lovely gesture; before I left for my meetings in Princeton…"

(Backwards time-traveling to Amelia's memory. Are you ready? Is the time-traveling going OK for you? Feeling all right? Good, then let's go!)

CHAPTER 10 -

Bridezilla Revealed

December 19, morning
*COUNTDOWN TO CHRISTMAS: 25 24 23 22 21 20 **19** 18 17*

Amelia opened the door to Teddy and Pip's room, her cell phone in her hand, looking anything but amused with them. "Boys! Please!" she said, in a tone much more harsh than her usual sweet voice. "I was *trying* to have a *conversation* with a *person* about my *wedding!* All of your carrying-on is not helpful!" As soon as she said it, Amelia felt terrible. What kind of person was she becoming, shouting at furry little guinea pigs?

Teddy lowered his eyes guiltily, but Pip continued to run up and down ramps yelling at the top of his little voice, wheeking in his most siren-like style, and knocking things around whenever possible. In addition to all of this, the TV set was on very loud. Pip had chosen a game show with plenty of clappers clapping, cheerers cheering and buzzers buzzing.

*"AMELIA, IT IS TIME TO **NOT** TALK ON CELERY PHONES! IT IS TIME TO BE WITH BEST FRIENDS PIP AND TEDDY!"* Pip was still shouting, taking a moment to stop running and take a sip of water. *"WE WANT YOU TO*

READ TO US! WE HAVE HAD NO READING IN DAYS AND MONTHS! NOT EVEN A PAT ON THE HEAD HAVE YOU GIVEN YOUR BEST FRIENDS..."

"Oh, Pip..." Amelia's tone softened immediately. "Darling, I know I have been distracted and... I am very sorry; I truly am, but..."

"NO! BUT IS NO GOOD! NO BUT!" Pip shrieked. *"'BUT' IS NOT WHAT WE NEED TO BE HEARING FROM YOU NOW! OR EVER!"*

"I have an appointment this morning in Princeton!" Amelia called over his shrieking. "I have no choice, boys, it is an appointment with my sister and the wedding planner and then..."

"Is Wedding Planner the new best friend?" Teddy asked quietly. *"And also this sister who does not like guinea pigs? Is that the new Best Friends Club? And me and Pip are not in it?"* Teddy's voice was full of sadness.

Amelia's heart felt like it was being painfully squeezed. She said nothing for a whole minute. Pip stopped his racket, even muted the TV. The guinea pigs waited.

"You two mean the world to me. I love you. It's just... the wedding," Amelia said with a sigh and a voice full of pleading. "I need to do some things..." she trailed off. "Just a few more things..."

"Amelia, you are Bridezilla," Pip said seriously. *"It is no good and you must fight the bad monster inside of you. The end."*

"I'm ... I'm what?"

"Bridezilla is scary lady wedding monster. This bad thing happens to nice good people," Pip explained. *"Teddy and me, we see this on TV, so it is true."*

"Pip is watching much TV... lately," Teddy supplied with a shrug. *"He learns new things."*

"Style TV, channel 70," Pip said. *"We were surprised to find that our very Amelia is this monster thing. We are not enjoying this."*

"Oh, darlings…" Amelia began, but just then, the phone rang in the other room. She looked vaguely at her cell phone, realized it wasn't ringing, and then headed to the living room to quiet the other phone.

At this point, Pip re-started his previous tantrum. The TV volume went up and things began to be shoved around, causing as much racket as before.

Amelia managed to get their door closed just as her cell phone, too, began ringing.

Ten minutes later, she opened the door, both phones in hand, and approached them.

"You have appointment," Teddy said as Pip began to quiet down. *"Back when it is dark outside. Maybe Molly Jane will come and feed us, if you remember to ask her, or someone else might come… someone who does not love us."*

Amelia's eyes filled with tears. "I am so sorry," she whispered, setting the phone down before reaching out to scoop Teddy up and cradle him gently in her arms. "I do apologize, my darling Teddy. You deserve much better than this."

"Do you know that it is Christmas time at Molly Jane's house?" Teddy asked. *"There is a pretty tree with lights and there is music and… other things. It is some nice. Pip would be more good, or less bad, if there was just a little more regular for him. He is upset and feeling the feeling of neglected. And also irregular. Teddy feels like this too."*

Amelia kissed the top of Teddy's head and nestled him against her cheek. "I know. And the thing is, Teddy, the really *ridiculous* thing is, I think Wally feels that way a bit too. He is the person I'm supposed to be doing all of this *for* and yet… crazy, right?"

"CRAZY!" Pip supplied, appearing from out of an igloo. *"AMELIA IS TOO MUCH CRAZY AND IT IS TIME FOR NO MORE! WALLY AND PIP ARE NEGLECTABLE AND UPSET! AMELIA IS 'THE GRINCH WHO STOLE OUR CHRISTMAS'!"*

Amelia set Teddy back down and scooped up Pip. "Oh, how I love you, my feisty little Pippen," she whispered into his little ear. "Do you believe me? Say you believe me." Amelia pet him and hummed a little Christmas tune.

Pip began to purr loudly, and then sang, *"Amelia, Amelia, Yes I believe Amelia,"* in a soft sweet voice, a voice much different from the yelling voice he'd been using all day. *"But be careful because you are still on the thin ice,"* he whispered.

But this tender moment, as all were lately, was ruined by a loud knock on the apartment door. Amelia said some frustrated words that she normally wouldn't, set Pip down again and went to answer it.

"Amelia? Darling! We are SO LATE!" said the grating voice that the guinea pigs now knew all too well as Evelyn's. "My car is running and I am not at all sure it is legally parked, so for heaven's sake, let's go!"

And then Amelia was gone.

(Psst! Readers, it's me, Molly. We are going to do a really short time travel now, but to a different track. We need to go forward a couple of hours, but to a memory of mine this time. This one will be a little bit tricky, so make sure to have your seat belts securely fastened. Ready?)

CHAPTER 11 -

Daddy Brings Christmas and Joins the Club

December 19, evening
COUNTDOWN TO CHRISTMAS: 25 24 23 22 21 20 **19** *18 17*

Daddy and I hauled two big boxes up the steps, set them down and then unlocked Amelia's door. We were greeted by lots of wheeking and squealing from Teddy and Pip. When they realized it was me, they stopped wheeking and started to yell and scream instead.

"Molly Jane! Where is our dinner! We are hungry! Amelia leaves us, once again, with no food and we are HUN-GRY!" Teddy complained. *"What did you bring us? Why are you not giving us our dinner?"*

"I OBJECT!" Pip added, pushing Teddy so he was closer to me and first in line for food.

"Guys, cool it, okay? I have your veggies right here, I just have to put down some stuff…"

"STUFF IS NO GOOD, WE WANT VEGGIES!" Pip screamed. *"GUINEA PIGS DO NOT EAT THAT THING CALLED STUFF! THIS IS NOT THE TIME FOR JOKES AND TRICKS MOLLY JANE!"*

"Molly Jane, who is with you? I smell a new-person smell, and we have done the talking!" Teddy squealed. *"Uh-oh!*

This is a big uh-oh Molly Jane! Is it a person who will make us do the job of research?"

"No, it's fine! It's my dad. Daddy is here to help me with a little surprise that I thought of for you and Amelia. It is a surprise that you will love, I promise. It's okay, Daddy knows about your talking."

"Molly Jane, is this person you are talking of called 'Dad Jane'?" Teddy asked, scratching his head.

"Nope, just 'Dad'," I giggled. "Jane is my mom's… it's a girl's name. Daddy's name is Dan."

"Can we call him Dad Jane?" Teddy asked, standing up to peek out the doorway. *"So there is matching between all of you people?"*

"Uh…"

Then Daddy walked in with his big box. Both guinea pigs stopped all noise and moved close together, looking nervously up at him.

"Hey there… little guys," Daddy said a bit awkwardly. "Molly here tells me that you like Christmas…"

"There is no Christmas at our house. Amelia stole it and shoved it up the chimney," Teddy informed him, still moving his head from side to side, trying to see what it was that he was bringing into their room.

"Amelia is Bridezilla," Pip said softly, *"but you will not catch that bad thing, if you are not a girl. Apparently."*

Daddy looked at me, scratched his head a little, then looked back at the guinea pigs, "Molly and I are bringing a little bit of Christmas up here for you." He started opening up his box. "Molly will take care of your dinner while I set up this little tree…"

"Dad of Molly Jane is bringing a Christmas tree to us?" Teddy squeaked happily. *"I was not knowing that Christmas could come to us in that very box!"*

"WE LIKE BOXES!"

"The worst of times changes to the best of times! And even better of times is dinner… Molly Jane, where is our…"

I set down the food bowls and the two of them started to munch away, their eyes focused constantly on what Daddy was doing.

Daddy is totally allergic to furry animals of all kinds. He was very brave to be up there with me and I gave him a happy smile and two thumbs up. Before we came upstairs, he took some medicine called an antihistamine so he would not get snuffly and stuff. So far, he was doing fine.

Daddy put the little artificial tree in the corner of the room where Teddy and Pip could see it best. Then he strung the lights and I started with the ornaments. Teddy and Pip watched everything, quietly. I showed them each ornament before I put it on the tree. They liked the ones that were shiny and showed their reflections.

Well, the whole thing turned out totally beautiful. We all looked at it and felt happiness all around us. I popped a Christmas CD into Amelia's player while Daddy strung even more lights around the doorway and windows. The guinea pigs stayed amazingly quiet, watching with their eyes big and bright as their room became more and more magical and Christmasy.

"I am going to help you guys make the coolest Christmas card for Amelia and Wally," I told them. "I brought over my digital camera. I will take a bunch of pictures of you two, and then Daddy will turn the picture into a card after we choose the best one. But... first, I need you to try on something I made in Girl Scouts."

Both guinea pigs backed away, and Pip yelled, *"GIRL SCOUTS IS NO GOOD! THAT THING IS NOT ABOUT CHRISTMAS AND WE ARE NOT GOING TO DO IT... WHATEVER IT IS! I OBJECT! DO NOT SPOIL THIS HAPPY TIME MOLLY JANE!"*

"Molly Jane, surely this is not the time of Squirrel Snouts Stuff..." Teddy said, more reasonably than Pip.

I pulled two red felt stocking caps out of my box and held them out to Teddy and Pip. "Hats," I explained. "These are Christmas hats, so they *do too* have to do with Christmas. I made them for you at my last Girl Scout meeting. We just have to fasten them under your chins with this strap… it shouldn't be that uncomfortable… please, guys?" I begged as they both backed away from me. "It will be *such* a cute picture! Think about Wally and Amelia and how happy they will be to see the picture… only five seconds, okay?"

Teddy and Pip were both up the ramp and hiding in the farthest corners before I could finish my sentence. I could hear Daddy chuckling and saying something like "…told you so…" Of course this did not help matters at all.

After a lot more begging and the promise of extra lettuce if they would cooperate, they allowed me to tie the little hats under their chins, but only until the count of ten. I did not think I could take too many pictures in ten seconds, but it was better than nothing.

They realized right away, though, that the hats had jingle bells on their tops. Both guinea pigs started shaking their heads around wildly.

"Molly Jane! You make jingle-bell hats for best friends Teddy and Pip!" Teddy said happily. *"Maybe the scouting is good for one thing!"*

"JINGLING HATS ARE MUCH MORE FUN THAN NOT JINGLING HATS!" Pip squealed, running around, tipping his head from side to side. *"WHEEE!"*

When they finally were able to stand still for a few seconds, I took some pictures. I chose the best one and Daddy went back to our house to print it out for us.

"While Daddy is off doing that, I am going to read you a Christmas story called *The Night Before Christmas*," I said, pulling the book out of my box and sitting in the wheely chair by Teddy and Pip. "Have you heard this story before?"

Teddy and Pip shook their heads, bells jingling as they did so. *"Is it Best of Times, Worst of Times?"* Teddy wanted to know. *"Was it a story that was made up by our Dickens?"*

"Nope, it's a totally different story. It's about Santa Claus."

"Santa Claus is good. We would like to hear it," Teddy said.

"I LIKE SANTA CLAUS! HE IS MUCH GOOD!" Pip screamed. *"MOLLY JANE READ!"*

Here is how that went:

The Night Before Christmas – Guinea Pig Style

"'Twas the night before Christmas and all through the house,

Not a creature was stirring, not even a mouse...'"

"MOLLY JANE! STOP! OBJECTION!"

"What's the matter, Pip?"

"Mice are no good."

"Make the story about guinea pigs," Teddy said, shaking his jingling head. *"Okay Best Friend Molly Jane?"*

"But this isn't a story I'm making up, it's a really old story, written in the 1800s by Clement Moore, and this is how it goes," I said, reasonably. "Besides, mouse rhymes with house, which was in the first line..."

Reasonably does not usually work on Teddy and Pip. Their jingly heads were shaking firmly.

"No mice."

"MICE ARE NO GOOD! GUINEA PIGS ARE NOT STIRRING! CHANGE IT!" Pip said in his screamy way.

I looked at them for a minute, then, trying not to laugh, started the story over.

"'Twas the night before Christmas and all through the house,

Not a creature was stirring, not even a ... guinea pig...'"

"Molly Jane, I changed my mind. I do not like the sound of not even *a guinea pig—it sounds no good,"* Teddy informed me.

"WORST OF TIMES! GUINEA PIGS RULE!" Pip screamed.

"Not even a human person, that would be better and not hurt our feelings," Teddy said.

I looked at their serious expressions, then took a deep breath and started over again.

"'Twas the night before Christmas and all through the house,

Not a creature was stirring, not even a human being;
The stockings were hung by the chimney with care...'"

"MOLLY JANE! STOP! OBJECTION!"

"Pip, what's the matter now?"

"STOCKINGS ARE FOR FEET. HUMAN FEET ARE NO GOOD. THEY ARE STINKY!"

"Come on, you guys must know about Christmas stockings! That's what this is talking about. It's a tradition. You hang them by the fireplace and Santa fills them with good stuff. You don't use real ones; people don't wear those kinds of stockings on their feet."

"Are you sure, Molly Jane?" Teddy asked seriously. *"Because it would be very no good for Santa if he had to touch and put things into stinky feet stockings."*

"I'm sure," I said.

"But some no-good person could put the fireplace Christmas stocking onto their smelly feet?" Teddy continued.

"Well, I guess..."

"OBJECTION!" Pip squealed. *"NO GOOD!"*

"Okay, guys, in this story, no one puts the stockings on their feet, ever. I promise."

They were quiet for a few seconds, then nodded solemnly, jingling their hats.

"Can I continue?"

"Go."

"'In hopes that St. Nicholas soon would be there...'"

"MOLLY JANE! STOP! OBJECTION! WHO IS THIS NICHOLAS?!"

"St. Nicholas is another name for Santa Claus."

Silence.

"Okay, go," Teddy said, settling down comfortably to hear the next line.

"MOLLY JANE! READ THE STORY!" Pip yelled.

"'The children were nestled all snug in their beds,
While visions of sugar plums danced in their heads,
And Mama in her kerchief...'"

"MOM JANE IS NO GOOD! THIS STORY IS NOT ABOUT MOM JANE!"

I ignored that, and went on:

"'...and I in my cap,
Had just settled our brains for a long winter's nap—
When out on the lawn there arose such a clatter...'"

"MOLLY JANE! STOP! OBJECTION! THE STORY IS BEING SCARY NOW!"

"Pip, it's not scary, the clatter is..."

"Do not say it Molly Jane! You will lose the surprise for us!" Teddy squealed.

"TOO SCARY! STOP MOLLY JANE!"

"Well... should I keep going?" I asked, not sure which of them to listen to.

Pip was actually hiding his eyes. Teddy was nodding yes.

"Pip is a scaredy pig. Do not pay much attention to him."

"'...I sprang from the bed to see what was the matter.
Away to the window I flew...'"

"Molly Jane —human people do not fly. This story is not possible," Teddy interrupted, shaking his jingly head. *"Flying in the house for a grown-up human is no good anyway."*

"Okay, what that means is he walked fast, or maybe he ran. They don't mean 'flew' like flying like a bird."

Silence.

"Okay? Can I keep going?"

Nods and jingles.

"'Away to the window, I flew like a flash,
Tore open the shutter

and threw up the sash…'"
"Threw up sounds no good."
"OBJECTION!"
"It means he opened the window."
"Molly Jane, it is Christmas in the story, and it is cold and winter. Open the window is a bad idea. Guinea pigs will be cold."
"The… well, the guinea pigs are in a different part of the house, the open window was in the bedroom of the dad."
Silence.
"MOLLY JANE! READ THE STORY!"
"'The moon on the breast of the new fallen snow,
Gave the luster of mid-day to objects below…'"
"Molly Jane? What does that thing mean? It is no-good talk, makes no sense."
"WORST OF TIMES!"
"It just means that the snow was bright in the moon-light…"
"DON'T CARE," Pip said, shaking his head.
"Not important. Please only read important parts, Molly Jane," Teddy said, sitting down with his head on his paws. *"We want to hear only about Santa Claus."*
"That's the next line, okay? Hang in there guys…
'When what to my wondering eyes should appear,
But a miniature sleigh, and eight tiny reindeer…'"
"MOLLY JANE! STOP! OBJECTION!"
"I object too!" Teddy squealed. *"What means the tiny and the miniature? Santa Claus is not tiny or miniature. Tiny miniature reindeer and sleigh would not work. This is no good. Santa is some fat and would break a tiny sleigh."*
Pip nodded his vigorous agreement and his hat jingled crazily.
"I can't answer that one, guys, I don't know why the writer said that the sleigh and reindeer were small. They aren't. Maybe they seemed small from way up in his bedroom window."
They considered that for a moment.

"REINDEER ARE NO GOOD! THEY EAT GUINEA PIGS!" Pip shrieked.

"No. I am sure they do not," I said, turning back to the story.

"They do and we will not hear of them anymore. Take them out of the story, please," Teddy said firmly.

"Teddy, not you too! Come on, you guys! No way! Now you are messing with the whole entire story of Santa Claus! He has reindeer—that's the way it goes!"

"REINDEER EAT GUINEA PIGS—NO GOOD!"

"I can't take them out of the story," I said. "Let's just believe, between us tonight, that these reindeer are the best possible kind and they do not eat anything except reindeer feed, which is wheat or grain or something."

Silence.

More silence.

Then, finally—*"Okay."*

"OKAY MOLLY JANE—READ THE STORY! WHY DO YOU KEEP STOPPING?"

"'…With a little old driver, so lively and quick…'"

"I know, they say he's little, but we know he's not—can I keep going?" I said quickly.

Nods.

"'…I knew in a moment, it must be St. Nick.'",

"That's the same as Santa Claus," I added quickly.

"We know that, Molly Jane, why are you telling us things we know already?" Teddy said.

Nods.

"'More rapid than eagles his coursers they came,"

I heard Pip very softly saying, *"Eagles are no good,"* but he did not stop me this time.

"'And he whistled and shouted and called them by name;

"Now Dasher, now Dancer…'"

"MOLLY JANE DO NOT SAY THE NO-GOOD REINDEER NAMES! REINDEER EAT GUINEA PIGS AND THEY ARE WORST OF TIMES!"

I stopped reading and turned the page, trying to guess what it would be that they objected to next.

"Do you guys do this when Amelia and Wally read stories to you?" I asked with a giggle.

"Oh yes. We surely do," Teddy said, nodding.

"And they change all the words around for you?"

"Much of the times. Not all. Some stories have too many words and much of them are not for us to understand anyway. Some, like Christmas stories, we have much understanding and they need to not hurt our feelings or scare us out of our little heads."

"I see," I said, reaching out to pat Teddy's little head under his jingle hat. "I'll see if I can fix the story as we go so there will be no hurt feelings or scared... ness. Okay?"

"BEST OF TIMES! NOW READ!" Pip demanded. *"I LIKE THIS STORY!"*

"Skipping... skipping..., um... 'With the sleigh full of toys – and St. Nicholas too...' Skipping... 'Down the chimney, uh, Santa Claus, came with a bound:'" I ended up skipping two whole pages because they mentioned the reindeer.

"See! Santa Claus makes a bound... that thing means big sound for big person - not miniature."

"'He was dressed all in fur from his head to his foot,

"MOLLY JANE! SANTA IS GOOD AND WOULD NOT WEAR A COAT THE SAME AS NO-GOOD EVELYN!" Pip yelled.

Dang, I missed that one!

"'And his clothes were all tarnished with ashes and soot;

A bundle of toys was flung on his back,

And he looked like a peddler just opening his pack...'"

Somehow, we got through the story. It took a very long time.

"How about this? Let's sing some Christmas carols!" I suggested.

"Carol is not what we want to do, let us sing songs instead!" Teddy said excitedly.

"CAROLS ARE WORST OF TIMES! CAROLS ARE FIRED!"

"Carol is what they call this kind of song. It's the same thing. But, okay, we'll call them songs. How about jingle bells? You guys can jingle your hats!"

They seemed to be excited about that. I started the song:

"Jingle bells, jingle bells, jingle all the way...
Oh what fun it is to ride in a one-horse open sleigh...."

And then the objections started.

"HORSES ARE NO GOOD! NO HORSES! Horses eat guinea pigs," Pip squealed.

"Pip... they do not eat guinea pigs. Horses are vegetarians."

"Molly Jane, it is best not to talk or sing of horses around my Pip. He is afraid of those things and cannot be talked out of it," Teddy said quietly. *"We need to have the word changed."*

"Okay... how about guinea pigs can be pulling the sleigh?"

"WORST OF TIMES!"

"Guinea pigs do not pull heavy things for humans to ride in. That is no good. Plus, it is impossible. We are not strong."

"What if they were really big strong guinea pigs?"

"Nope, still no good. Our feelings would be hurt about having to pull a sleigh. It is no good. Please do not say guinea pigs."

"Maybe we should sing something else..."

"NO! WE SING JINGLE BELLS! IT IS THE RIGHT SONG FOR OUR JINGLING HEADS!" Pip screamed, which made me kind of get the giggles.

"How about a magic flying sleigh?" Daddy had walked back into the room with the finished Christmas card and was chuckling as he joined us.

Teddy and Pip stared at him for a while and then nodded, jingling their hats. *"Dad has found the answer to our sleigh problem! Dad is very cool! We will say magic flying sleigh and this will not scare us or hurt our feelings."*

"Thanks Daddy," I said grinning at him. "Shall we start again?"

"Jingle bells, jingle bells, jingle all the way,
Oh what fun it is to ride in a magic flying sleigh—eh,
Jingle bells, jingle bells, jingle all the way,
Oh what fun it is to ride in a magic flying sleigh.

Dashing through the snow, in a magic flying sleigh,
O'er the fields we go—laughing all the way—ha ha ha!
Bells on guinea pigs ring (now hats were jingling wildly)
Making spirits bright,
What fun it is to ride and sing a sleighing song tonight!"

"Hey, why don't you guys tell *me* a story, huh? You must know a Christmas story," I said.

"We will tell of THE Christmas story. The best story of all," Teddy said quietly. *"The baby in the manger story."*

Pip nodded eagerly, jingling his hat like crazy.

It went like this:

"Once upon a time in a place called Bethlehem, the much much good people called Mary and Joseph came to town because the bad people made them go there for no good reason that we know of."

"NO GOOD—WORST OF TIMES! NO-GOOD PEOPLE MADE THEM RIDE THERE ON A DONKEY IN WINTER TIME!"

"When they got to Bethlehem, which is not close to New Jersey at all, they tried to stay in a nice hotel but there was no room. People were neglecting them. They had nowhere to stay. Human beings were being no good."

"BUT ANIMALS WERE BEING BEST OF TIMES! THEY MADE A PLACE IN A GOOD STABLE FOR MARY AND JOSEPH AND THEN THERE WAS BABY CALLED JESUS WHO IS THE GOOD OF ALL TIMES, AND HE WAS IN A MANGER ON TOP OF HAY, WHICH IS MUCH MUCH GOOD, AND ANIMALS TOOK CARE OF HIM. ANIMALS ARE GOOD. EXCEPT SHEEP ARE SMELLY!"

"And there was a star of the brightest bright and it was shining over the stable and then humans called shepherds came, they are the boss of the sheep, and they stared at the baby. The angels sang good songs (not carols). Then kings came."

"KINGS BROUGHT NO-GOOD GIFTS! BABIES DO NOT NEED GOLD; THEY NEED FUZZY BLANKETS AND RATTLES! WORST OF TIMES…"

"All was good. Baby Jesus came to be the best in the world and the animals saved the day. The end."

"THE END!"

What could we possibly say to top that? We smiled.

The card turned out great. The picture of Teddy and Pip in their Christmas hats was adorable! On the inside, I wrote this note:

Dear Amelia and Wally, I am so happy that you are close to me and my family. I hope we will always be that close. Teddy and Pip love you very much! Have a great Christmas! Molly

"Dad of Molly Jane brings Christmas to sad neglected guinea pigs, so he is now in Best Friends Club!" Teddy declared, standing at the bars near to my dad. *"We are thanking you. Can we call you the name of Dad?"*

Daddy chuckled and looked at me, then back at Teddy. "It's not every day a guy gets asked that by a … uh… a fine gentleman like yourself. I would be honored."

"CAN WE CALL YOU 'DADDY-O'?" Pip squeaked.

Daddy said, "Um…"

Teddy giggled. *"Can we call you 'O'Daddy-O-Daddy-O'?… Tee hee!"*

"TEE HEE!" Pip giggled. *"CAN WE CALL YOU THE NAME OF RUMPLESTILTSKIN? TEE HEE HEE HEE!"*

"We are doing jokes and tricks with you," Teddy giggled. *"We like Dad-of-Molly-Jane-who-is-not-called-Dad-Jane."*

"DAD IS BEST OF TIMES!" Pip announced. *"BUT NOT MOM JANE! MOM JANE PUTS US IN A BUCKET AND CALLS US MONSTERS. DAD NEVER PUTS US IN BUCKETS! HE BRINGS CHRISTMAS. PIP HAS NO OBJECTION!"*

"Not so fond of being in a bucket, eh? Can't say I blame you for that. But Jane is okay, really, I kind of like her. I married her, you know."

"Our Best of Times Dad had a wedding with Mom Jane?" Teddy sounded shocked. *"Was Mom Jane Bridezilla? Was wedding worst of times?"*

"No, of course not... well, there were some tense moments, you know. It's always a big deal, a wedding. Girls get their ideas in their heads really early in life and then when it's time to do it for real, they just have to make it all fit into the dream they've always had, you see... sometimes it's really tough."

Teddy and Pip stared at him.

"I think for the ladies, planning the wedding is like... well, for example, I built that house we live in," Daddy said, pointing out their window toward our house, which was sparkling with Christmas lights and had electric candles lighting the windows.

"Dad is builder? Like HGTV guys? Dad truly is best of times!" Teddy proclaimed.

"Well, I planned it all; I didn't exactly build it all myself. There was a lot to decide, every little thing. It took me a really long time. I wanted to do it all right, just perfectly, because it was really important to me. I think ladies want their wedding to be like building the perfect house."

"But wedding is just a day and house is forever. And house is where you live with Molly Jane and Mom Jane for days and days, and that is some important," Teddy said reasonably. *"It seems like no good to have wedding planning like building a house."*

"Well, when you put it that way..." Daddy scratched his head. "I guess it's just a girl thing. We guys can't always understand it." He shrugged. "Molly? Any insight here?"

I shrugged too, as I was removing the jingly hat from Teddy's head. "I don't get it either, but I'm not planning on getting married ever, so I don't have those wedding dreams in *my* head. I think it's crazy to plan so much that you aren't having fun or anything. Not that I'm being mean to Amelia or anything. I would never do that."

"We guys," Teddy whispered. *"We are cool guys just like Dad!"*

"Well, *guys*," I giggled, "I think we need to get going. We don't want to be here when Amelia gets home, I want it to be a surprise for her. I really hope Amelia and Wally like what we did in here," I said, giving them each a final pet. "I'll be back tomorrow."

"Good night best friend Molly Jane and new best friend Dad!" Teddy squeaked. *"We are thanking you with all of our happy hearts!"*

"CASE CLOSED!" Pip shouted, as he allowed my allergic-to-everything-Daddy to pet him. *"COME BACK AGAIN! WE LIKE YOU!"*

(Ready to go back to the present, readers? Hold on tight, here we go................)

CHAPTER 12 -

What About the Cell Phone?

Back to December 22, evening
COUNTDOWN TO CHRISTMAS: 25 24 23 22 21 20 19 18 17

Amelia dried her eyes with a sleeve. She was laughing and crying at the same time. "Oh my goodness! Oh Molly, what a story! Aren't they amazing? And the way they do that word-changing thing when you read to them..."

Wally was doing his warm chuckling and shaking his head. "The boys are most certainly particular about wording. It makes it a great challenge to get through a book."

"Thank you, Molly, for the idea and for bringing Christmas to our home! Remind me to thank Dan again, will you Wally? The apartment was *awfully* desolate before the two of you came over. It means so much, really," Amelia said, reaching out to grasp my hand.

"Amelia, I really loved it; it was fun! I honestly thought that they were a lot happier afterwards," I added. "They were, right?"

"They were. Oh my, yes, they were! When I returned home later and walked into the room and saw it all... I was so pleased, and we had a really lovely evening together," Amelia said.

Mom was clearing her throat now. I could guess why. She thought the guinea pigs were totally not the point and we should get back to the problem and Evelyn and... whatever. So far we had talked more about Teddy and Pip than about the fact that the wedding was cancelled and what to do about it.

"Amelia? Can you remember the last time you had your cell phone?" Mom asked. "The fact that someone called your sister from your own phone, which is missing, seems pretty important to figuring this all out."

Amelia thought for a minute. "I was talking to Sunny, probably, on the cell phone, and then the *other* phone rang. I was supposed to meet Evelyn... and I was talking to Teddy and Pip in their room. They were so terribly upset with me! I might have put my cell phone down by..." Amelia stopped talking and looked at Wally.

Mom looked from Amelia to Wally and then to me.

I shrugged.

"I need to speak to Molly for a moment," Wally said, mysteriously, getting up from the sofa and heading to the kitchen.

I followed; eager to hear what he had to say.

"I made a promise *not* to tell Amelia about a certain phone call I received on the evening in question," Wally said, keeping his voice very quiet. "But I will tell you, Molly, for I fear it is relevant to our mystery. The call was from Pip. And he was indeed calling me from Amelia's cell phone."

I couldn't even help how loud my gasp was. "Are you serious?" I said. "Oh my gosh! How did this happen? Wally, this is *my fault!* I did it again! I messed things all up without even knowing I was doing anything! *I* showed Pip how to use a cell phone!"

(We are going to take a quick trip back to one of Wally's memories... ready?)

CHAPTER 13 -

A Phone Call

December 19, late afternoon
COUNTDOWN TO CHRISTMAS: 25 24 23 22 21 20 **19** *18 17*

> *"Wally, this is your Amelia... the wedding is a bad idea, and we need to do the eloping. I am now Bridezilla and it is no good..."*

"Pip?"

"...Wally?"

"Pip, what in heaven's name..."

"Wally? Best friend Wally! How are you? Nice day?"

"Pip? Are you calling me... from Amelia's cell phone?"

"Amelia says Pip can play with this celery phone for a day! It is no big deal, all is good," Pip said in his squeaky way. *"Good times! How are you, Wally? Nice day?"*

"Amelia would not leave her cell phone with you to play with, Pip, we both know that is true... what is going on?"

"It IS SO true! Amelia puts this thing by me and leaves with icky Evelyn! Pip knows how to use it from watching too much TV and Pip is me... but lately it is not so much fun to be... me... so I am calling my best friend Wally. How are you, best friend Wally?"

"Pip, tell me that you did not make any other calls before calling me," Wally said.

"I made a new song, just for you, Wally, listen to this... Jingle bells, Teddy smells, Christmas is no good..."

"Pippen?"

"Why is there no Christmas here at our house, Wally? Molly Jane has a tree and ornaments and songs and cookies and presents... we have nothing but wedding stuff and meany Evelyn. I object. Wally, you will come tonight and sing Christmas music to Pip and Teddy?"

Wally sighed. "Ah, yes, my dear fellow, Christmas. I do know how much you boys love Christmas. I also know that this is a really difficult time for you and Teddy. Your whole world is upside down and you are feeling left out. However, I am afraid that I cannot make it any easier right this minute as I am spending the evening with Amelia. Tomorrow, perhaps. Shall we plan on tomorrow?"

"Wally is with Amelia? Uh-oh. This is uh-oh. Please best friend Wally do not share with Amelia the secret that Pip is talking on her celery phone... okay? Thank you."

"A secret, is it? Well, I am not sure that this is a secret I should keep, Pip."

"Please Wally, please please please please keep this secret for Pip! Best friends sometimes keep the secrets for each other, sometimes. I think they do. Maybe Pip was a little much wrong about what Amelia says about this celery phone when she leaves it by me and then... you know that I object."

"Sustained. All right. You win this time, but you must make a promise. As soon as we say our goodbyes, you must hang up the phone, Pip. Can you do that? Just close it up and the call will stop. We don't want to drain Amelia's battery."

"We don't? No battery means no ringing. That would be better or best of times. I object to the ringing very much!"

That comment actually made Wally chuckle. "Ah, yes, but... no, we don't. It was actually mighty nice to talk with you Pip, thank you for calling."

"Mighty nice to call you Wally on celery phone. Please come soon and do best friend things with us. Teddy and Pip are watching too much TV and are on each other's very last nerves."

"Gotcha. Good night my friend."

"Got you too. Good night best friend Wally—who will keep my secret for me."

(Back to the present…)

CHAPTER 14 -

Pip in the Interrogation Chair

Back to December 22, late evening
*COUNTDOWN TO CHRISTMAS: 25 24 23 **22** 21 20 19 18 17*

"Oh… my… gosh," I breathed. "Wally, I don't believe it. But I think I do believe it. What have I done?!"

"Molly, no one will or would *ever* blame *you*, if this is truly the work of Pippen," Wally said quietly.

I shook my head over and over again.

Wally sighed. "Perhaps you will join me in a little conversation with Teddy and, especially, Pip?"

I didn't need to be asked twice. While Wally was telling Mom and Amelia… *some*thing, I put on my coat, boots, and all that winter stuff.

Following Wally, I hurried across the yard to the apartment. I was going over it all in my head and it made a super crazy kind of sense. Pip or Teddy made the calls. Most likely, Pip. They were very upset for a long time; they wanted to stop the wedding. In their minds, the sister and the wedding planner were the 'bad guys'… and they needed to be fired, so they fired them. Holy cow! Wow. Man oh man.

(This was great!)

As usual, Teddy was glad to see me and greeted me with a happy voice. *"Molly Jane! You are here to play and sing and read to us more!"* Teddy squealed with delight as I stepped into the room. *"Hooray! Oh and best friend Wally is here too! Hooray hooray!"*

"Good evening gentlemen," Wally said, approaching them and pulling up the chair. "I wonder if we could have a little talk?"

As soon as he said that, Pip ran away up the ramp and hid in an igloo.

Teddy came up close, his little feet gripping the bars. *"Sure thing Wally. I would like very much to have a talk, little or big, either is good for me. Pip? Why are you doing no manners with Molly Jane and Wally?"*

Pip did not say anything, or reappear.

Teddy shrugged and then settled down comfortably. *"What do you want to talk about, Best Friend Wally? Okay, I'll start. Pip is acting the thing of crazy,"* Teddy said. *"I do not understand. But, then, he is Pip. It is part of his being."*

"Teddy, my friend, it appears that phone calls were made, from Amelia's cell phone, to certain individuals. And now... well, our wedding is cancelled," Wally said calmly.

Teddy was completely silent. He stared at Wally, then at me. Then his little head started to slowly turn toward the upper ramp where Pip was peeking *his* little head out of the igloo. Teddy said in a whisper, *"Pip did that no-good thing... that is why he is being crazy... this time. But I was not knowing..."*

"Teddy, is there something that you *do* know, anything for sure?" Wally asked.

"There was a day, not so many days ago, when Amelia put down her sell phone in our very home here and left with no-good Evelyn for her long-time appointment. She left that thing here and Pip went to play with it very much. I took a nap and did not do anything wrong. The end." Teddy stretched and yawned. *"What else can we talk about, Best Friends?"*

Wally gave Teddy's head a pat and scratched gently behind his ears. "I feel that I need a word or two with Pip before we move on to the next topic, my fellow."

Wally stood up so he could get eye to eye with Pip. "Pippen, my dear fellow, I believe it is time for you to tell *your* side of this story." Wally peeked right into the igloo. "Come on now, you will not be in trouble. I am sure that your intentions were of the purest. Tell us what happened. Frankly, we are very impressed! Aren't we Molly? We would like to know all about it just because it is so impressive."

"PIP IS PLEADING THE FIFTH AND WILL NOT TALK WITHOUT A LAWYER PRESENT!"

"I will lawyer for you, crazy Pip," said Teddy. *"Now come down from there and tell our best friends how and also why you did the no-good thing before you are in trouble for even more reasons."*

"I OBJECT!" Pip screamed. *"This is being guilty before being proven... I mean... I... oh darn. I would like a new lawyer. BAILIFF, TAKE HIM AWAY!"*

"Pip," Wally's voice was soothing and gentle. "I understand. I believe I understand why. You may be interested in knowing that, it seems, you have achieved your goal. And, by the way, there is no danger of us moving to Manhattan, that was a misunderstanding. We will all be staying here or very near to Molly, so please put that worry out of your mind. Please come out and talk to us Pip."

Teddy did some whoops of joy at the news about not moving, and Pip peeked out of the igloo.

"Come on, Pip! Come on cutie!" I encouraged. "Come down and tell us how you did it! You are such a smart *cool guy!*"

There was a moment of silence, and then Pip spoke. *"IT WAS WORST OF TIMES! AMELIA WAS BRIDEZILLA AND FORGOT CHRISTMAS AND REALTORS WERE CALLING AND NO-GOOD EVELYN WAS ALWAYS*

*AROUND PINCHING HER NOSE AND CELERY PHONE
WOULD NOT STOP RINGING AND MOLLY JANE WAS
BEING TOO MANY NIGHTS AT SQUIRREL SNOUTS!"* Pip
squealed, coming all the way out of the igloo. *"SO PIP
SAVED THE DAY! And here is how it happened..."*

(Readers, fasten your seatbelts again, we are about to
zip back in time to relive Pip's memory!)

CHAPTER 15 -

Pip and the Celery Phone

December 19, right after Amelia left with Evelyn
*COUNTDOWN TO CHRISTMAS: 25 24 23 22 21 20 **19** 18 17*
For a while, Teddy and Pip did not say anything. They stood side by side looking at the empty doorway. Finally, Teddy sighed. *"It will all be done soon, right Pip? The wedding will happen and then there will be some normal."*

"Never normal, not really," Pip said quietly, sitting with his head on his front paws. *"There will be moving away to feel bad about. No more Molly Jane. Teddy, what if there is this wedding and Wally is not wanting to be in it? The Best Friends Club will be only Amelia, the no-good sister and Wedding Planner. And the celery phone."*

"Pip, I know that these times are worst, I do know this and agree with your feelings and feel them too, but I do not think that there can *be a wedding with no Wally in it... and also a celery phone cannot be in Best Friends Club because it is a machine. And finally, it is not a celery phone; celery is crunchy and much fun to eat. It is SELL phone, like... shopping. Humans call it that thing because they do their talking into it while they are in stores... I think."*

Pip wasn't listening; he was walking very slowly to where Amelia had, amazingly, left behind the least-liked new member of the Best Friends Club. The celery phone.

At first the only thought in his mind was to hide the hated object. Bury it in the bedding. Then he thought, maybe, he would find a way to turn it off. That would be good. Pip approached it carefully, checking over his shoulder to see if Teddy was watching.

Teddy had curled up in a cushiony bed and was napping.

It took some work to open the phone up. It had been easy for Molly Jane with her long human fingers, but for Pip's short legs, it was difficult. Pip pawed and nudged at the opening with his nose until, finally, it sprung wide open, revealing a tiny screen with a picture of the two of them on it, and a set of shiny, glowing buttons.

Teddy, who had already finished his nap, wandered over to see what it was that had made Pip so quiet.

"Amelia's sell phone?" he whispered. *"Uh-oh. Pip, what are you going to do? It is not for chewing... no pottying on that thing!"*

"This is not uh-oh. This is Pip saving the day. Pip will bring back best of times," Pip said quietly.

Teddy sighed and put his head down. *"It is a good thing to say, but Pip, guinea pigs cannot change the things that people are doing."*

"Pip will do it! Teddy can go do other things while Pip saves the day. It is secret spy work and you are better to not know of it."

"Okay, Crazy Pip, do your no-good crazy spy work. Teddy is going to nap very very much."

"Pip can do a celery phone very good," Pip said, as he started pushing buttons with his foot. Finally, a screen came up with a list of words. Pip did not know what the words were, but when he pushed one of them, numbers appeared

and then the celery phone started to make a far-away ringing sound. Somewhere in the world, another phone had started to ring. Pip listened hard until he heard a voice. "This is John Riley, of HomeLand Realty… I am unable to take your call, but please leave a message at the beep…"

"First, we fire The Realtor very much…" Pip whispered. *"Crazy no-good realtor wants Pip to talk after he says the word of 'beep' so that is what I will do. I am saving the day…"* When he heard the beep, he said, in his best court-room judge voice… *"This is Amelia's best friend calling you. There will be no moving. We do not want to buy any real estate at all. Moving from our home would be worst of times. Thank you and good bye."* Pip stomped on the red button next to the number buttons until the celery phone was quiet once again.

Having succeeded in that firing, Pip moved on with confidence. He pushed more buttons, fired more people, in fact, fired everyone who picked up. Many of them were rude, most were confused. But it didn't matter. It was much much fun.

"Hello?" said the complete stranger.

"You are fired. Have a nice day! Tee hee!"

"Who is this? Hello? *Hello?*"

After a few more anonymous calls, he heard the familiar voice of Sunny, the no-good wedding planner who was taking his Amelia away and causing her face to do frowns so many times. Like the realtor, she had not answered her phone, but a recording of her no-good voice told Pip that she would, of course, get back to him as soon as possible. Pip did not want her to get back to him; he wanted her to go away. He waited for her beep, and then said: *"This is Amelia. I am sorry but I have to fire you. The wedding is a bad idea and it is making my life worst of times. Do not call me again ever. I will tell Wally that we are going to do the elope plan and have no big wedding. Fire everyone and cancel everything. Do not call me. Thank you and sorry. Goodbye and good luck. Sorry to fire you. Have a nice day."*

Pip was having a lot of fun. Not only was he solving all of the problems, he was powerful! He pushed buttons, fired whoever answered, and left messages on machines all over the civilized world.

But then, quite by accident, he chose the combination of buttons that attached him to the celery phone of Mr. Walter Holmby. He began to leave a message but ended up hearing the live voice of Wally himself.

(Back to the present!)

CHAPTER 16 -

The Jury is Out

Back to December 22, late evening
*COUNTDOWN TO CHRISTMAS: 25 24 23 **22** 21 20 19 18 17*

"Wow," I said, honestly impressed.

"Pippen, I ... I surely do not know what to say, exactly," Wally said, rubbing his chin, his expression somewhere between shock, amusement and confusion.

"As lawyer for Pip," Teddy began. *"I say that Pip is not so smart to know how to really do the firing and cancel of weddings. He was being upset and did a no-good thing, but did not think it would really work for real. I would suggest a small amount of time in a minimum security prison."*

"OBJECTION! PIP IS SMART AND SAVED THE DAY! TEDDY IS A NO-GOOD LAWYER!"

"I am inclined to agree, partially, with Teddy. Meaning that Pip's intention was simply to blow off steam, and not to cause utter chaos. Pip, is that correct? The fact that the people involved took it all so seriously and that this has spiraled into the misunderstanding that it has... well, we can hardly blame a feisty little guinea pig for all that, can we?" Wally asked.

"WE CANNOT! WALLY IS SAYING THE RIGHT THING!"

"Molly? Any thoughts?"

I was a little surprised to be consulted on this. "Um... well, Pip didn't mean to, or expect to cause all the trouble. I mean, when you think about it, if a lady got a message in Pip's voice, she wouldn't think right away that it was Amelia disguising her voice or anything like that, would she? The first thing you'd think was... I have no idea, actually. But I think there must be some reason that Sunny went to Evelyn about the call and that Evelyn got all upset and came to me, and then took everything *I* said the wrong way and then believed that Amelia did this, or that I did it for her."

Wally and the two guinea pigs were staring at me.

"Hey, I'm just a kid, but I think that maybe Amelia kind of *wanted* things to stop, the wedding plans, I mean, because she wasn't happy with the way it was going. I'm sorry, but her sister is real scary and bossy and I don't know about the wedding planner..."

"WORST OF TIMES!"

"Wedding planner is some scary, too, Molly Jane!"

"I guess I think she must be *bossy* too. Maybe they actually *knew* that Amelia wasn't happy and they made her feel like she couldn't stand up to them. So when Pip did his thing, they assumed that it was actually Amelia trying to get out of the plans... you know?"

Wally was nodding thoughtfully. So were Teddy and Pip.

"Anyway, that's what I think," I finished with a shrug. "I think Evelyn bossed her sister into a big huge wedding in the city and Amelia wanted something different. So maybe Pip *did* save the day after all... in a way."

Wally kept on nodding. "Perhaps. And, perhaps, we can even find a way to use this 'salvation' to our advantage," he said. "I think it's time to call together the whole Best Friends

Club. Perhaps your parents have some thoughts, or some strings they can pull…"

"Mom Jane is not in Best Friends Club, Wally," Teddy pointed out quietly.

"MOM JANE IS NO GOOD! SHE CANNOT COME!"

"Pippen, you are not really in a position to be critical of… *anyone* right now. All right, fellows, I will amend that statement," Wally said with a shake of his head. "Let us call together the Best Friends Club plus Molly's lovely and helpful mother… let us see if perhaps we can re-plan a wedding for Amelia… one that *is* completely to her liking."

CHAPTER 17 –

Wedding Bells and Jingle Bells

Christmas Eve
COUNTDOWN TO CHRISTMAS: 25 24 23 22 21 20 19 18 17
'*Silent Night, Holy Night…*' the music was soft and the fireplace crackled. Snow lightly fell outside the window. Father Tim from our church stood by the Christmas tree, holding a book and smiling. Wally stood near to him, facing the entryway, waiting. He was dressed in a very handsome black tuxedo. Daddy stood next to him, in his best suit, tugging at his tie every ten seconds.

At Mom's signal, I started walking toward them in my red velvety dress and shiny black shoes. The shoes were totally pinching my feet. I carried a big white basket with a red bow on top. In it, on top of a red velvet cushion, were Teddy and Pip, wearing black top-hats and bow ties.

Mom sat in one of the white folding chairs that we had borrowed from the church, next to Amelia's and Wally's parents. Wally's younger sister and her family sat in the next row of chairs. Next to them were some of Wally's friends from Princeton. The rest of the chairs were filled up with my Grandma Club. My grandmas were so excited to be there, I can't even tell you!

And then Amelia walked in. She was so beautiful. Everyone kind of stopped breathing for a minute, especially Wally. Amelia looked like an angel in her white gown and long flowing veil. She carried a bouquet of red roses. Teddy and Pip were whispering something, careful not to let the non-best-friends in the group hear them. It was clear that it was all good stuff, though. I wanted to kiss the tops of their little heads, but of course I couldn't because of the hats—and well, I was the maid of honor, I had to save my guinea-pig-kissing for later.

So who would've thought in a million years that the wedding of Amelia Dearling, famous novel writer from New York City, would be held in *my* living room, on Christmas Eve and with only twenty people there, plus her two guinea pigs? Well, it was. It was totally cool.

After all of Pip's 'beans had been spilled', we had sat down and had a meeting with Amelia, Wally and my parents to talk about a new wedding. Teddy and Pip were there, and had promised to only listen unless someone asked them for their ideas. It didn't exactly work that way, but we did manage to have our say in between their comments.

After telling us that she *had* actually been thinking about it *a lot*, and had been having a really hard time admitting it to anyone, Amelia told us that she had never wanted that big fancy wedding at all. She had no wish to be surrounded by crowds of fans, publishers, editors and all those types of people. She wanted her wedding to be filled with only people who loved her and Wally the most. Then she told us that she had always had this image in her mind, of getting married on Christmas Eve by a Christmas tree. (She got the idea from the wedding in the movie *Santa Claus is Comin' to Town*. You know, that really old Christmas show where Santa marries Jessica? They get married in the woods with only animals for guests… oh and those Kringles too….) Amelia said she was a bit embarrassed that *this* was her wedding dream, but we all encouraged her to go for it—especially me. Having Teddy and Pip at the ceremony made all the sense in the world with a dream like that. Amelia told us that she had told Evelyn early in the planning process that she wanted Teddy and Pip to be part of her wedding. Evelyn had a real big fit and Amelia had backed down.

Things got really busy after the meeting. We made lists and divided up all the things that had to be done. The first thing was that Amelia and I headed out and got Christmas presents for Teddy and Pip, because she said it was really important. That was so fun! She actually bought Pip a karaoke machine. She got the first book of the *Harry Potter* series for Teddy, though she said she wasn't quite sure how reading that book to the guys was going to go. She also got a really nice framed picture of the Best Friends Club for both of them. We went to the local pet store and picked out new cozy beds and blankets, some things to chew on and a big bag of extra good hay. I wrapped and hid all of this while Amelia went back out with Wally to get his tuxedo.

Daddy said he thought our parish priest would be able to stop by to do the ceremony, as long as it wasn't too close to any stuff he had to do at church that day. He got right on the phone and made the call. Mom knew someone who could whip up some flowers for Amelia to carry and also knew that the church had a bunch of white chairs. Once that was settled, we had to move a lot of furniture around to fit the chairs into our living room. We even had to move our presents out from under our tree. Our living room was not built for holding weddings, exactly, but by the time we were finished, it looked like it was.

Mom and I went shopping to get a dress and some new shoes for me. I do not enjoy shoe shopping, or wearing dresses, but… it was for a good cause.

While we did that, Amelia and Wally went right down to the good old Westerfield grocery store and bought an already-made wedding cake. I offered them two guinea pig figurines that I think look like Teddy and Pip to put next to the bride and groom at the top of the cake. Mom thought it was very inappropriate, but Wally and Amelia thought it was a wonderful idea.

I was also in charge of guinea pigs; outfits and transportation. I found the big white basket and put the bow on it, and also found the velvety pillow and some hats at the local craft store. With Daddy's help, I gave the guinea pigs quick baths and comb-outs the morning of the wedding. They were pretty good about it, considering. I ended up needing a bath myself once it was over, but I would have had to take one anyway, so it was fine.

My only complaint about how things turned out, was that Tweets was not invited to the wedding. I tried *really* hard to get Mom to change her mind, but she said it would be even more inappropriate than the guinea pigs on top of the wedding cake. Poor Tweets.

So, in less than two days, the Best Friends Club planned Amelia's whole wedding. The wedding dress was the only thing Amelia kept from the first wedding. She had to, because it was perfect. There was no question about it. I think it would have made Evelyn crazy to know how simple and quick it all was.

Amelia told us that she was a little bit sad that Evelyn wouldn't be there for the Christmas Eve ceremony after all. The two of them had been through a lot the past few months with all the planning, and had maybe, somehow, gotten closer. Then, she thought for a minute and changed her mind. She said she realized, now, that she and her sister had such *totally* different lifestyles and ideas about things, but she was relieved to find that they *could* still love each other anyway. Besides, Amelia knew it would be a huge disappointment to Evelyn, to see how totally different Amelia's wedding was, compared to what they had been planning together. So it was probably best that Evelyn was over in London. Nobody disagreed with that.

Mom came up with a pretty great idea, actually, to possibly cheer up Evelyn about the whole thing. Wally and Amelia are going to write her a long letter explaining everything, and agree to have a big reception party later in January and invite all of those fancy people who were originally coming to the wedding. That way, all they have to do is send out a new invitation to them with a different time and place—or something. I don't know. Evelyn can figure it out. She is going to be able to do all the planning herself. Amelia and Wally will just show up, for only a few hours, and then they will get back to their life, which they love, in the suburbs of New Jersey.

Amelia and Wally made phone calls to their family and closest friends and were very happy that some of them could be there with so little notice on Christmas Eve. Since it was only a few people, I asked if I could invite some more. I invited the grandmas, making super-cool fancy invitations for them, and handing them out personally. Daddy rented a big van so we could pick them up and then drop them all off at their different Christmas Eve places once the ceremony was over.

After the wedding, we had a reception with just punch and cake. People stood around the living room talking and stuff. Wally and Amelia's moms and all of my grandmas took turns holding Teddy and Pip, who behaved extremely well. We had a signal between us; if either of them had to "go" they would get my attention with three quick wheeks. That way I could scoot them off to the litter box and nobody would get peed on.

I think the sweetest part of the whole wedding was when we had cleared away the chairs and put on some dancing music. Of course Wally and Amelia danced, and then the parents and all that mixing up stuff—and then Amelia took Teddy and Pip and cuddled them to her and she danced slowly around and around. Even my mom had to smile.

CHAPTER 18 –

A Happy Ending

Christmas Eve
*COUNTDOWN TO CHRISTMAS: 25 **24** 23 22 21 20 19 18 17*
　　　"Molly Jane, we are much happy to be sleeping over at your house this night. It is our first ever slumper party and it is much fun," Teddy said, as he rearranged the bedding in the portable cage that Wally had set up in my room. *"We will wait anxiously for doing the thing called slumper."*
　　　"SLUMPER SOUNDS NO GOOD!"
　　　"It's slumber, actually," I said with a yawn. "It means to sleep."
　　　"This party is about sleep? That is no difference than our usual lives," Teddy slumped down disappointed. *"I feel that we have been tricked."*
　　　"WORST OF TIMES—MOLLY JANE IS TRICKING US!"
　　　"I love you guys," I said, reaching out to pet them. "Even though you are difficult sometimes. I need to *SLUM-BER* because it is Christmas, you see, and tomorrow if I get some sleep there will be presents to open!"
　　　"Santa is coming!" Teddy shrieked. *"Molly Jane, I almost forgot that thing! Pip and Teddy will do much slumber right away."*

"MOLLY JANE, NO SCARY REINDEER WILL COME INTO THIS HOUSE TONIGHT AND EAT GUINEA PIGS... IS THAT RIGHT?!" Pip ran to hide in the nearest igloo.

"I promise you, the reindeer have never come into the house, and they won't do it tonight," I said with another big yawn. "You're safe. I'll be right here if you need anything."

The two guinea pigs nodded, standing side by side watching me as I got into bed. My parents would be coming up soon to tuck me in and read *The Night Before Christmas*. I was pretty sure that there would be commotion when that happened, and my parents would not be too happy about having to change all the words to the story. I giggled at the thought of it. Maybe it would be better to go downstairs and have them read it to me by the fireplace tonight.

"Molly Jane, will you tell us a Christmas story?" Teddy asked.

I smiled. "Honestly, I'm all worn out, guys. Telling you a story is kind of a lot of thinking. But I do have an even better idea. How about you guys tell me a story?" I said, throwing a blanket over my shoulders and sitting next to the cage.

They looked at each other, whispered something and then Pip began his story in a calm and quiet voice.

"Pip will tell the true story of the worst of times that are now done...

Pip's Christmas Story

Once upon a time there was a Best Friends Club. It was best of times. Best friends Wally and Amelia were doing the wedding thing and had plans. But there was a no-good sister and planner and bad bad celery phones. Soon and very soon there was neglecting of best friends Teddy and Pip. Pip did much TV-watching and also screaming. Teddy did some screaming too. It was not working. Molly Jane Fisher, best friend, was too busy with being a grade-fourther and the doing of the homework and playing of the piano to fix the problem and save the day. Max was no help. Mom Jane is still no good.

Then one day, things got even worse. Teddy and Pip got the bad thought in their worried small heads that best friends Wally and Amelia were talking to realtors about going far away from other best friend Molly Jane Fisher. Plus also they had stolen our Christmas. Mostly Amelia, who was now Bridezilla. It was the worst of times.

Then one other day, the dad of best friend Molly Jane came to visit and brought Christmas. He is now a best friend. The time was good. There were scary stories and Christmas trees and lights and jingling hats.

But before this Christmas-good happened, there was a day of not good, when Pip did a thing that… was good and saved the day. But most others did not think the same way. We do not need to talk about it. It saved the day and all is well.

No-good planner is gone. Celery phone does not work anymore. No-good Evelyn is in the place of London so she can have best of times and worst of times with Mr. Dickens. The wedding was best best because Teddy and Pip were there in fancy hats with Molly Jane. There was a basket and velvet and we were just like kings. Maybe now we are *kings. Plus also Amelia was the thing of beautiful and Wally was handsome and there was smiling all around. And now we have many grandmas who are much sweet and cuddling of us.*

Amelia and Wally best friends are now the thing of married. First they need to be some alone for one night. Teddy and Pip were brought to the room of Molly Jane Fisher who is going to protect us from the guinea-pig-eating no-good reindeer while we wait for Santa to bring us good things because we have been very good. Some of the time.

The end."

Merry Christmas to all,
and to all a good night!

Pip's Christmas Hits

HATS HAVE BELLS
Christmas is good when best friends are near.
I am happy Molly Jane is here.
Christmas is best when hats have bells.
Joy to the whole world, my heart swells!

Dad brings Christmas to Pip and Ted-dy.
Tree and lights and music and glee.
Christmas is best when hats have bells.
Joy to the world... Pip's whole heart swells!

NO CHRISTMAS AT OUR HOUSE
(extended version)
There is no Christmas – at our house,
There are no lights and no tree.
There is no Christmas – at our house,
no Christmas for Teddy and me.

There is no Christmas - at our house,
no presents or stockings to see.
There is no Christmas - at our house,
we want to come live with Mol-ly.

There is no Christmas - at our house,
no jingle bells jing jingle-ly
There is no Christmas - at our house,
we want to come live with Mol-ly.

There is no Christmas - at our house,
It got stuffed right up the chimney.
There is no Christmas - at our house,
we need to come live with Mol-ly.

GRUMPY JINGLE BELLS
Jingle bells,
Christmas smells,
weddings are no good.
Wally never visits us
and Amelia is the Bridezilla... who stole our CHRISTMAS!

THE WEDDING IS NO GOOD (I MISS AMELIA)
Amelia, Amelia, oh how I miss Amelia.
The wedding is no good.
Wedding Planner is no good.
Oh how I miss Amelia.

I BELIEVE AMELIA
Amelia, Amelia, Yes I believe Amelia

The Night Before Christmas – Guinea Pig Style

Twas the night before Christmas and all through the house,
not a creature was stirring, not even a human being;
The stockings (which were never worn on stinky human feet)
were hung by the chimney with care
In hopes that Santa Claus soon would be there;
the children were nestled all snug in their beds,
while visions of sugar plums danced in their heads.
And Mama (who is not Mom-Jane) in her kerchief, and I in my cap,
had just settled our brains for a long winter's nap—
when out on the lawn there arose such a non-scary clatter,
I sprang from my bed to see what was the matter.
Away to the window I walked quickly and opened the window to *my*
room,
not the guinea pigs' room, and tore open the shutters.
The snow was bright in the moonlight (enough said).
When what to my wondering eyes should appear,
but a regular-sized sleigh,
and eight regular-sized but extremely nice non-guinea-pig-eating
reindeer,
with a regular-sized old driver, so lively and quick,
I knew in a moment, it must be Santa Claus.
(We will not speak of the reindeer.)
Santa Claus got himself onto my roof.
Down the chimney Santa Claus came with a bound:
He was dressed all in fur (not made from animals!) from his head to
his foot
and his clothes were all tarnished with ashes and soot;
a bundle of toys was flung on his back,
and he looked like a peddler just opening his pack:
His eyes – how they twinkled! His dimples were nice,
his cheeks were red and so was his nose.
His regular-sized mouth was smiling and his beard was white.
He had a pipe but he did not smoke it because smoking is no good.

He had a broad face, and a regular-sized round belly
that shook when he laughed, like a bowl full of jelly.
He was chubby and plump, a right jolly old elf, and I laughed when I saw him,
which was bad manners.
A wink of his eye and a twist of his head soon gave me to know I had nothing to
dread.
He spoke not a word, but went straight to his work,
and filled all the clean never-worn stockings, then turned with a jerk.
And laying a finger aside of his nose and giving a nod, up the chimney he rose.
But I heard him exclaim ere he drove out of sight —
Merry Christmas to all, and to all a good night!
(Whew!)

For more fun with Teddy and Pip, go to
www.teddyandpip.com

Breinigsville, PA USA
15 December 2010
251493BV00001B/116/P